ROY CLINTON

NATIONAL BESTSELLING AUTHOR

BAD TO THE BONE

A MIDNIGHT MARAUDER ADVENTURE

BAD TO THE BONE

A Midnight Marauder Adventure

Roy Clinton

Published by Top Westerns Publishing (www.TopWesterns.com), 3730 Kirby Dr., Suite 1130, Houston, TX 77098. Contact info@TopWesterns.com for more information.
Book Design by Teresa Lauer: Info@TeresaLauer.com.
Cover by Laurie Barboza DesignStashBooks@gmail.com
Copy Editor: Sharon Smith

Substantive Editor: Maxwell Morell

Other Books by Roy Clinton

Lost
Midnight Marauder
Return of Midnight Marauder
Revenge of Midnight Marauder
Midnight Marauder and the President of the United States
Love Child
Candy Man (to be released in the second half of 2019)
Missing (scheduled to be released in early 2020)

These books and others can be found on
www.TopWesterns.com and *www.Amazon.com.*

Audio versions of the books can be found on
www.Audible.com as well as on iTunes and Apple Books.

Dedicated to
Richard "Dick" Barnes
Who just saddled up for his final ride
You will be missed as a beta reader
Keep ridin' cowboy!

Table of Contents

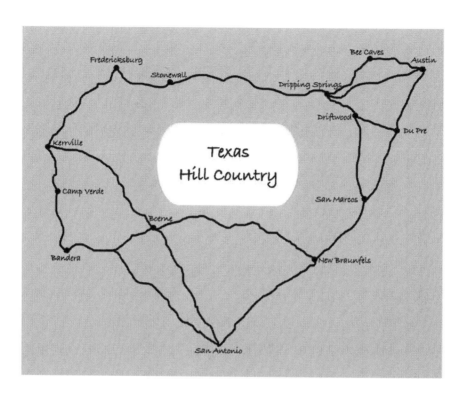

PROLOGUE

May 1874
BANDERA, TEXAS

Please don't hurt my husband anymore." Thelma Jackson watched in horror as Butch "The Butcher" Granger stomped on her husband's hand. Jack Jackson shrieked as he pulled back his mangled paw.

When Granger spoke, his top lip was pulled back exposing his teeth. He appeared to have a permanent smile. His hair was gray and matted to his head. His long sideburns were bushy. While he didn't wear a beard, he did have a week's worth of whiskers that caused his face to appear dirty. Granger had big ears that stuck out from his head giving him an elf-like presence. His ample gut hung over his belt completely obscuring the buckle. Wide suspenders attached to his trousers accomplished the herculean task of keeping his pants up.

"Where is it? I know you have gold hidden on your ranch.

Everybody knows it. Old man you better tell me now. I'm runnin' out of patience."

"We don't have no gold, mister. I'm just a worn-out old farmer. I ain't never had more than fifty dollars to my name."

"Everyone in Bandera knows you're rich. You've been sittin' on a pile of gold all your life. Now where is it?" Granger took off Jackson's belt and looped it around Jack's other hand and dragging him roughly across the room. Thelma ran to her husband's aid and tried to pull the belt away from Granger. Butch pushed the elderly woman to the ground. As he stood over her, he took his six-gun from its holster, pulled back the hammer, and shot Thelma in the middle of her forehead. Jack cried out and tried to crawl to his wife.

"Thelma! Thelma! What have you done, mister? Why did you shoot Thelma?"

"You better tell me where your gold is or I'll kill you too."

Jackson let out loud wails as he looked at his dead wife. "All right. I'll tell you. There's a little strongbox buried in the barn. Please don't hurt me no more."

"Show me. Get up old man and show me where you have your gold."

Jack Jackson wiped his eyes as he stood. He walked over to the body of his wife and bent to kiss her. Granger savagely kicked the old man to the ground.

"I said show me where you buried the gold." Granger grabbed the belt that was still around the old man's hand and started dragging him out of the house.

"Please, mister, let me walk. I'll show you where it's buried."

Jackson got to his feet and staggered off the porch and across the yard to the barn. He walked to the back of the barn and pointed to a barrel. "I buried it under this here barrel."

"So, dig it up." Granger found a shovel and threw it at the feet of the old farmer.

Jackson used his uninjured hand to roll the barrel out of the way and began digging. After a few minutes, Granger lost patience with the slow progress, grabbed the shovel, and pushed Jackson to the ground. Granger dug down a little over two feet when the shovel struck the box containing the gold. Slowly, Granger freed the box from its hiding place. When he dragged it out of the hole, he opened it and found it filled with gold coins. On closer inspection, Granger realized the coins were all Double Eagles with dates from 1849 to 1866.

"How many you got?" Granger lifted out a handful of the Liberty Head coins.

"There are five hundred in that box and a few more in the cookie jar in the kitchen. That's over ten thousand dollars, mister. You can have it if you'll just ride away and leave me in peace."

"I can have it all right because it's mine now. And I'll be riding away just as soon as I put the gold in my saddlebags."

Granger took his gun from its holster and pulled back the hammer. With a sinister grin, he shot Jack Jackson twice in the chest. The Butcher retrieved his saddlebags, emptied them of the supplies he carried, and divided the gold coins between them. He guessed each bag weighed a little over fifteen pounds. Granger looked through the discarded supplies and retrieved the two sticks of dynamite he kept for so called "special occasions." He walked to the house, lit the fuse on both sticks, threw them inside, and ran back to the barn.

The explosion was deafening but Granger was not worried about being caught. He knew the closest ranch house was a couple of miles away. Even if someone heard the blast, he knew he would be long gone before anyone showed up at the ranch.

* * * * * * *

Butch Granger grew up in Bandera and was known for his cruelty. When he was only five years old, the marshal rode out to his parents' ranch and saw young Butch hacking up a dog with a long knife. The marshal swung down to scold the boy and discovered the remains of another dog. Granger's parents laughed it off when the marshal told them of their son's actions. "Boys will be boys," was all his father said.

No one seemed to recall Butch's given name. When he started school, the other kids called him The Butcher because of his fondness for killing pets. They eventually shortened it to Butch. The moniker stuck. Butch liked the name and the reaction of people when they found out about his fondness for murdering small animals.

Granger left town when he was fifteen. His parents died in a fire that was of suspicious origin. It was assumed Butch started the fire but in an absence of evidence, no charges were filed. As far as anyone knew, Butch Granger never again came to Bandera until he killed the Jackson's, blew up their home, and rode away with their life savings.

Roy Clinton

CHAPTER 1

Mayor! Mayor!" shouted Marshal Clem Williams as he galloped up to the headquarters of the H&F ranch. Clem continued shouting as Slim Hanson came out the front door.

"Marshal, what's so all fired important?" asked Hanson.

"Slim, I've just come from the Jackson's place. Someone blew up their house and killed Thelma and Jack."

"What? Who'd want to harm that old couple? They never harmed anyone. I don't think they have any enemies at all."

"Seems they've got at least one," said the marshal.

"Let's ride back to their place, Clem. Are their bodies still there?"

"They were when I left a few minutes ago."

Slim saddled his horse and yelled out to his foreman, Owen, that he was leaving with the marshal. As he saddled up, the marshal was already urging his horse into a fast gallop. Slim fell in behind him and they rode due east as hard as they could. It took about twenty minutes to get to the Jackson's place. Slim was horrified as he looked at what was left of the demolished house.

"It looks like someone dynamited their home," said the marshal. Slim and Marshal Williams swung down, tied their horses at what was left of the hitching rail, and walked gingerly through the pile of lumber that used to be a house. "Thelma is over there a ways.

"How'd you find out about the murders?" asked Slim.

"Well, I was in my office when ol' lady McKeever rode her buggy up and shouted for me. I went out to see what the ruckus was about and she told me she heard an explosion out east of her place. She said it sounded like someone was starting a mine. Well, I knew there weren't any mines around here but decided I needed to find out what the explosion was all about. I really thought ol' lady McKeever was just hearin' things. But I rode out and figured I'd just stop by each ranch I passed and ask if anyone had heard anything strange. The Jackson's place is just east of McKeever's so I rode there first.

"I saw the house was blown up and could see Mrs. Jackson in the wreckage. I could tell she was dead. I mean, look at her Slim, her body is torn up worse than what a bobcat would have done. Then out in the barn, I found Mr. Jackson. He was shot twice. That's when I rode over to get you. The H&F was closer than town and I didn't want to waste any time getting' someone else to see how I found the bodies."

"There's nothing we can do for Thelma," said Slim as he looked down at her lifeless body. It looked to Slim as if she had her back to the explosion. He gently turned her body over so he could see her face.

"Clem, come look at this. Someone shot her in the forehead. She didn't die from the explosion."

"Then why would anyone blow up the house if she was already dead?"

"I don't know, marshal. But whoever did it is just bad to the bone. Someone has a mean streak in him that's a mile wide. Let's go out to the barn and see where you found Jack."

Marshal Williams led Hanson out to the barn. They found Jack Jackson lying on his back. He had two bullet holes in his chest. Beside him was a shovel, a deep hole, and an empty strongbox. Slim knelt beside Jackson's body and stared at him. It was as though he was looking for any sign of life.

"Here's what they were after," said Slim. "There have been rumors for years that Jackson had a stash of gold. I didn't pay any attention to it 'cause Jack has never done anything but farm. There's not much money in raising corn and oats so I figured that was an idle rumor. But it looks like he did have money and buried it right here in his barn."

"Who would do this?" asked the marshal. "It just don't make any sense to me. I don't know anyone in Bandera who would do such a thing. It had to be some stranger who rode out this way."

"But a stranger wouldn't have known about the rumors that the Jackson's had a stash of gold," said Slim.

Slim stood and went over to the empty strongbox. There was an assortment of items beside the box that didn't look like they belonged. Slim found some beef jerky, a can of peaches, a beaten-up coffee pot, a hunk of bacon, and an envelope containing a letter.

The letter had a return address for Louise Granger of San Antonio, Texas.

"What have you got there?" asked the marshal.

"It looks like someone emptied his saddlebags here so he could pack up the gold he stole from Jackson," said Slim. "And there's a letter here from someone in San Antonio named Granger. I've only known one person named Granger but I haven't seen him in at least twenty-five years. And he's...."

Slim's mouth dropped open as he read who the letter was addressed to: Butch Granger.

"Butch Granger was the meanest kid I ever met. I went to school with him and he was always gettin' into trouble. He liked to kill. Butch would kill any dog or cat he found. When he was just into his teens, his parents died in a house fire. Everyone knew Butch did it but there was never any proof. I lost track of him after that. He dropped out of school and disappeared. But it makes sense that Butch could have done the killin'. We all heard the rumors about the Jackson's having gold hidden on their ranch. All the kids talked about it. There was even a time when several boys went over to the ranch with shovels to see if they could find what they called hidden treasure. As I recall, Butch was the one who put the others up to it."

"Do you really think he did the killin'?" asked Clem.

"I shor do. I can't imagine why anyone other than Butch would have a letter in their possession addressed to Butch."

"What's the address on the letter?" asked the marshal.

"It gives Butch's address as Kerrville. Marshal, I think we need to find out what is known in Kerrville about Butch. Let's hitch up Jackson's buggy and take their bodies back to town. As far as I know, the Jackson's don't have any kin around here. I guess we'll just talk to the undertaker and the preacher and get them buried in town."

Roy Clinton

CHAPTER 2

When they got to town, Slim drove the buggy to the undertaker's office. He went to the back entrance to try to minimize the spectacle of bringing in two bodies, one of which was badly mangled by the explosion. Slim paid for the funerals since there was no one else to take care of them.

From there he went to the church. The preacher was next door in the parsonage. Slim swung down, removed his hat, and walked up the steps and across the porch. Each step of his boots on the porch boards announced his presence. As he made a fist and reached to knock on the doorframe, the door opened and the parson stepped out.

"Afternoon, Mayor. To what do I owe the pleasure of this visit? You know it's not Sunday yet." The parson laughed at his own joke. Slim smiled slightly and got down to business.

"Howdy, Reverend. Jack Jackson and his wife Thelma have been murdered. I just delivered their bodies over to the undertaker."

"My word!" exclaimed the minister. "Who would do such a dastardly thing? They were likely the gentlest and sweetest couple I've ever known. They've never harmed anyone."

"I agree with you, Reverend. Evidently someone believed the rumor that the Jackson's had gold hidden on the ranch."

"I always thought that was a story school kids started just to have something to talk about. Slim, do you have any idea who did it?"

"I think it may have been Butch Granger. I found a letter addressed to Butch beside Jack's body. It looked like the murderer emptied his saddlebags as he loaded up whatever he stole from Jackson. That letter was in a pile of discarded trail supplies."

"I haven't heard that name in more than twenty-five years," said the minister. "Didn't he move away after his parents died in the fire?"

"Yes, he did. The letter was addressed to him in Kerrville. I haven't seen him since I was a teenager. Butch was cruel and mean. He reveled in getting into trouble. It was like life was a big game to him. But it was a game in which he was as cruel as he could be to both man and animal alike.

"One day when I was in the fourth or fifth grade, we were at recess and all of the other kids were playing chase or shooting marbles. I watched Butch coax a little dog over to him so he could pet it. I kept watching because I knew that wasn't like Butch to be kind to an animal. When the puppy got close, Butch petted it a couple of times then he drove a stick down the puppy's throat. The dog moved a few steps and died right there on the playground.

Butch threw his head back and gave the most blood curdling laugh I've ever heard. He was a wicked boy and it appears he's just the same or worse as an adult."

"That's horrible," said the parson. "I didn't know such cruelty was possible."

"Well, I need to get back to the marshal's office. Thanks, Reverend, for taking care of the funerals. I want to pay you for your services."

"That's not necessary, Slim. I'm glad to do whatever I can."

"Thanks, Reverend. But if it's all the same to you, I would like to give you something." Slim pulled out a ten-dollar gold piece and handed it to the parson.

"That's very kind of you, Slim. It is not necessary but it's very much appreciated."

Slim walked off the porch and mounted his horse for the short ride to the marshal's office. Marshal Williams was just coming out of the office when Slim arrived.

"Walk with me, Slim. I was just going to the telegraph office to see if there has been a reply to my telegram to the Kerrville marshal. I told him of the murders and said we suspected Butch Granger had a hand in it."

When they arrived at the telegraph office, there was a message waiting. The very anxious clerk gave the message to the marshal.

Marshal Williams
Bandera, Texas

Butch Granger suspected in murder of elderly couple in Kerrville. He also robbed the bank three weeks ago and blew up the safe. No leads on his whereabouts. Known to ride with three men: brothers Skyler and Morgan and another man.

Marshal Brodey
Kerrville, Texas

The marshal and Slim read the telegram together. "Marshal, it might be a good idea to contact the Texas Rangers and see if they have any information about Granger."

"I was thinking the same thing, Slim."

Marshal Williams dictated a message to the Texas Rangers headquarters in Austin. They didn't have to wait long for a reply.

Marshal Williams
Bandera, Texas

Butch Granger suspected in several bank robberies and murders in Texas Hill Country. No solid leads on his location.

Captain Jessup, Texas Rangers
Austin, Texas

After Slim and the marshal read the second telegram, they

walked without speaking back to the marshal's office. Clem put on a pot of coffee as the mayor took a seat.

"Marshal, I don't know what to do now. The Texas Rangers are after Butch so I don't know of anything else we can do."

As they pondered their next move, John Crudder rode up to the hitching rail and swung down.

"I'm not surprised I would find you two together," said Crudder. "How about a cup of that coffee I hear the marshal's famous for."

"Coming right up, John," said the marshal. "I just made a fresh pot. Slim and I were getting ready to have a cup."

"What are you two so gloomy about? You are acting like someone just died."

"That's exactly what happened, John," said Slim. "We have just come back from the Jackson's farm and found Jack and Thelma both dead. Someone shot Thelma in the head and blew up the house with her body still inside. Then we found Jack in the barn shot dead. He was lying beside a hole in the ground with an empty strongbox nearby."

John accepted his coffee and sat down on the other side of the office. "I just can't believe it. The Jackson's never brought any harm to anyone. I remember when Charlotte and I got married; they gave Charlotte a beautiful necklace that Thelma said belonged to her mother. She wanted Charlotte to have it saying she always felt like she was more of a granddaughter to her. And when the twins were born, she knitted several baby caps for each of them. I'm glad I came into town. When you didn't show up for breakfast, I figured somethin' had come up."

John married Slim's daughter three years earlier. Slim doted on his granddaughters Claire and Cora. Most mornings Slim would come over to have breakfast with John and Charlotte.

John looked at his father-in-law. "Any idea who killed them?"

"I think it was a fellow named Butch Granger," said Slim. "He was gone from here long before you came to Bandera. He was about fifteen when he left here. I think he's my age so he should be around forty-two."

"John," said the marshal, "we've just come from the telegraph office. Marshal Brodey in Kerrville said Granger is wanted for murder and for robbing the Kerrville bank. We also found out the Texas Rangers want him for other murders and bank robberies."

"Did Granger ride alone?" asked John.

"Well," said Marshal Williams, "there were two men named Morgan and Skyler. The Kerrville marshal thinks they were brothers. There was also another man but I don't recall his name."

John pondered what the marshal said. As he drank his coffee, he looked at his boots and contemplated what he was going to do. Slim and Marshal Williams exchanged a look and continued drinking their coffee.

"John, you have that look about you," said Slim. "What are you plannin'?" John continued looking at his boots, then took another swallow of his coffee.

"I'm not plannin' anything—at least not yet. I was just thinking how sad it is that the Jackson's are both dead. I'm gonna miss 'em."

"We all will," said Slim. "They were fine people. No one deserves to be treated like they were. There was no doubt what killed Jack. But what I didn't mention is that his right hand was crushed. It looks like Granger stomped on it several times. It probably broke every bone in his hand."

As John stared at the floor, Slim could see the muscles in his jaw and at his temple moving. No one spoke for a while. Finally, John stood and thanked Clem for the coffee.

"I better be gettin' home. I need to tell Charlotte I've decided to ride up to Kerrville to see what I can find out. Slim, I know you'll help Charlotte with the twins while I'm gone."

"Of course. You can count on it. I enjoy havin' Claire and Cora join me with my coffee in the mornings so Charlotte can sleep a little longer."

"How long are you gonna be gone?" asked the marshal.

"I don't rightly know. All I'm sure of is Granger has outlived his usefulness on this earth. I guess I'll stay 'til I take care of business."

"John, why don't you let me deputize you before you go," said the marshal. "That way, you have a legal right to hunt him down."

"Thanks, Clem. But if it's all the same to you, I'd rather not be carryin' a badge. As a private citizen, I have just as much right to protect people from Granger. And a badge just might get in my way." John turned and walked out the door onto the boardwalk.

Clem followed and shouted at John. "Now, John, I don't know if that's what the law says at all. Sworn officers of the law have the job of protectin' people. You should really take a badge with you."

John paused, turned back and looked at the marshal but didn't say anything.

"All right, John. Have it your way. But please be careful. We don't want to be losing any more good citizens of Bandera."

"You have my word, Clem. I'll be careful." Then turning to Slim said, "I reckon I'll be gone when you get back to the ranch. Thanks for watchin' out for the girls."

With those words, John untied Midnight, wheeled the great horse around, and headed south out of town. He wanted to get to the H&F as soon as he could. When he arrived at the ranch, Charlotte came outside to see who was riding up in such a hurry. She looked at John and knew instantly he was getting ready to take another trip. Although she didn't know the circumstances, she knew her husband would not stand by when there was an injustice that needed to be addressed.

John swung down and met her on the porch. He put his arms around her waist and tenderly kissed her. Then he pulled away and went inside to pack a couple of extra shirts and some clean underwear. Charlotte retrieved his saddlebags from Midnight.

"I'll pack some food for the trail," said Charlotte. "There's a side of bacon in the smokehouse along with some beef jerky I just finished yesterday. I'll also put in some flour, coffee, salt, and the biscuits left over from this morning." A tear came to her eye as she added, "I'll also put in the bottle of whisky, some bandages, ointment, a needle, and some sewing thread. And I noticed that you already have a pair of handcuffs and your shovel. I hope you get to use the handcuffs and not the shovel."

Charlotte hurried out to the smokehouse, gathered the meat, and returned to the kitchen to get the other supplies. John went out to the barn and got his ground cloth and a blanket and put his shirts and underwear in his bedroll. As he completed tying it to the back of his saddle, Charlotte came out of the house with the saddlebags close to overflowing. She caught the quizzical look John gave her.

"I didn't want you to go hungry."

"Charlotte, someone murdered the Jackson's."

Charlotte gasped and put her hand to her mouth. "That's awful, John. They were both so kind and gentle and the girls always looked forward to seeing them."

John took Charlotte in his arms again. "The man who did it must not have a conscience at all because he hurt them badly before he killed them. I have to go and stop him before he does this to anyone else."

"I know you do, John. And I know you'll be careful for me and the girls. Do what you need to do and then come back to us safely."

John kissed her firmly on the lips and walked out to his thoroughbred stallion. The tall horse stood in contrast to his petite owner. John grabbed the saddle horn, mounted Midnight, and immediately went into a gallop heading north.

Roy Clinton

CHAPTER 3

Kerrville, Texas

As he drew close to Bandera, John passed Slim. John pulled his hat off and waved at Slim and continued riding hard without any break in the rhythm. Slim returned the wave and continued toward the H&F.

John didn't want to have to slow down in Bandera so he took the trail that bypassed the town and continued to give Midnight his head. Any other time, John would be laughing as he saw how much his great horse loved to run. But his mind was on the cruelty of Butch Granger and how much he wanted to see him pay for what he had done.

Kerrville is about twenty-five miles north of Bandera. John knew he would easily get there before dark. After about twenty minutes of galloping at top speed, John put a bit of tension on the reins to signal Midnight to slow down. While he knew the strong horse could run like that for more than an hour, he didn't want to push him too hard. Most other horses would need to be reined in to slow them from a full gallop. But Midnight responded to the slightest touch from John. He was used to his rider letting him run hard at the beginning of a ride and then slowing for the rest of the journey.

A few miles out of Bandera, they came to a stream. John swung down and allowed Midnight to get a good drink. He pulled off his hat and filled it to the brim and drank his fill. With horse and rider refreshed, the journey to Kerrville continued.

By midafternoon, John arrived in Kerrville. Kerrville is located on the Guadalupe River in Kerr County. The county and the town were named for James Kerr who was an officer in the Texas Revolution.

John was surprised to find most of the businesses in town were owned by Charles Schreiner, Sr. In the center of town, Schreiner built a six-bedroom mansion for himself. It was the only building made of limestone in the whole county. Schreiner was said to be born of French nobility. He served time as a Texas Ranger but left the Rangers in 1857 to purchase a general store in Camp Verde, a frontier post the U. S. Army had established two years earlier. Camp Verde was about twelve miles south of Kerrville. Schreiner's success as a store owner enabled him to open additional stores and purchase a ranch in Kerrville, and get into banking and many other businesses.

Camp Verde was known for the forty camels the government brought in as an experiment to be pack animals that would extend the range of soldiers patrolling in the area. But the Army's horses and mules would bolt when they smelled a camel. Soldiers didn't react much better for they detested the smell of the animals.

John Crudder looked at the Schreiner mansion and thought of the grand home his father had built on Fifth Avenue in New York City. He was still reeling from the fact that unsavory characters had burned it to the ground a few months earlier and nearly killed his childhood nanny, Alvelda.

Crudder's painful memories helped him focus on making sure Butch Granger was not allowed to continue his reign of terror. Granger must be stopped and Crudder knew he could not rest until the menace had been addressed. What Crudder didn't know was if he would be called on to use his skills as the Midnight Marauder to deal with Granger.

If he could operate within the law to bring Granger to justice, he would do so. But he was also convinced that Granger needed to be stopped even if he had to step outside the law to make that happen. The Midnight Marauder felt he had a responsibility to keep people safe from those who preyed on others.

Crudder rode past the mansion and found the marshal's office. He swung down and tied Midnight to the hitching rail. John walked into the office but found it was empty so he walked down the street to Wild Willie's Saloon.

He spotted a man at the end of the bar wearing a badge and drinking a beer. John walked up beside him and said, "Marshal, could I buy you another beer?"

The marshal stood at well over six feet tall, a good foot taller than Crudder. John looked up at the marshal and saw him smile for a moment and purse his lips. Finally, he said, "Sure, little feller, I'll let you buy me a beer. Why don't we take a table over here? Willie, will you get us a couple of beers?"

John followed the marshal to the table and when they were seated, John extended his hand. "I'm John Crudder from Bandera."

"Pleased to meet you, John. I'm Marshal Brodey. Thanks for the beer."

"You're welcome, marshal." John waited until the bartender left their beers and then leaned over to the marshal and asked, "Why do they call this place Wild Willie's?"

The marshal smiled. "Ol' Willie used to be a mean drunk. He would come in here might near every week and drink heavily. And when he was good and drunk, he would get into fights. Before he was done, he'd not only broken some heads but several tables and chairs to boot. I would lock him up most Friday nights. The next day when Willie sobered up, he would pay for damages and I'd let him out of jail. He finally decided it would be cheaper just to buy the place."

"So now if he breaks something," said John, "he's not charged with destroying property."

The marshal smiled. "That's just it. Willie didn't know how much owning this place would change his life. Now he limits himself to only one beer in the evening and he refuses to serve anyone who's already drunk. This is now the best run saloon in town. But I'll bet you didn't come here to talk about the saloon."

"You're right about that. I used to be the marshal in Bandera.

In fact, Marshal Williams was my deputy."

"Then you must be here about Butch Granger."

"That's right. Marshal Williams told me he telegraphed you and you said Granger was wanted for murder and for bank robbery."

Brodey took a swallow of his beer. As he set it on the table, he frowned and wrinkled his brow. "Granger's lived here for maybe a couple of years. He's the meanest man I've ever known."

"Can you tell me about the murders he's wanted for?" asked John.

"Well he's wanted for one murder but I suspect he has murdered others," the marshal stated matter-of-factly. "He robbed the bank about two months ago and killed a clerk. Witnesses said he walked in the bank and wasn't even wearing a mask. It's like he didn't care who saw him. He demanded the clerk open the vault but the clerk said he didn't have the combination. They had just had a new vault with a Yale lock installed. The clerk really didn't know how to get into the safe. Granger said he would teach him how to get in the lock. He tied the clerk to the handle of the vault and lit three sticks of dynamite and blew the door off its hinges. There wasn't much left of the clerk."

"Did he have some grudge against the clerk?" asked John.

"No. He didn't even know him. Granger is just mean like that. About a year earlier, he got in a fight at another saloon in town. The other man pulled a gun on Granger. It didn't take long for Granger to disarm him. Instead of letting that be all, Granger repeatedly stomped the gun hand of the man he was fighting. I've never seen such a messed-up hand."

"I'm guessing you arrested him, right, Marshal?"

"I shor did. He was tried for battery. The judge gave him thirty days in jail and fined him fifty dollars. The man he stomped so badly ended up losing his hand. All through the trial, Granger just sneered. It was like he was happy at what he had done."

"Marshal, you said there were other murders you think he committed. Can you tell me about them?"

"People or animals?" asked the marshal.

John was stunned by the marshal's question. Brodey looked up and shook his head in disgust as he recalled the cruel things Granger had done.

"We know for a fact Granger has killed many dogs and cats around here. I can't tell you how many children have come crying to my office to say they saw Granger kill their pets. My deputy and I went out to tell him of the complaints. He just sneered at us. As we rode off, we heard a shot so we turned back and watched as Granger grabbed the legs of a dog he had just shot and dragged it behind his barn. John, there was a stack of carcasses there of maybe twenty or thirty dogs and cats. I don't know what to make of a man like that. That's not even human."

John shook his head as he considered what the marshal told him. More than ever, John knew Granger needed to be stopped. "So, what about the people he murdered?"

"Well, before Granger came to town, I don't recall there ever being a murder in Kerrville. But soon after he got here, an elderly couple who lived several miles out of town were murdered. There weren't no evidence Granger did it but it just seemed to fit him."

"How do you mean?" asked Crudder.

"Someone reported hearing shots and then an explosion near the couple's ranch. We found the old man outside of his barn. His hands had been tied with wire behind his back. They were tied so tight that the skin was broken and his hands had already turned black. The old woman had been stomped somethin' fierce. Her hands and feet were a mess. They had been crushed. She must have been in terrible pain."

"How did he kill them?" asked John.

"He shot them both in the head. I have often wondered if he made the old man watch as he murdered his wife." The marshal had a visible shudder as he recounted the horror of the scene.

"Why do you suppose he killed them?"

"John, I've been studyin' on that. It don't make sense to me. I guess he was lookin' for money. The house was pretty well torn up. Someone had gone through it like they were lookin' for somethin'. But that old couple didn't have any money. They were as poor as a church mouse. Everyone knew they didn't have nothing to speak of. I think Granger might have just wanted to hurt someone and the old couple was handy."

"You mentioned an explosion."

"Yeah, there was an explosion. He dropped a stick of dynamite down their well and threw another into the barn. One wall was blown out of the barn but the well was ruined. Why would he want to do that? He just ruined it so no one else could ever use the well."

"From the little I have known about Granger," John said, "it does sound like his handiwork. You said there were some other murders?"

"There was an old drunk that used to hang around town and bum drinks off anyone who took pity on him. He never harmed anyone but he did make a nuisance of himself by begging for food and drinks. About a year ago, he was found beaten to death behind a saloon at the other end of town. I wasn't sure what was used to beat the old sot. There wasn't any obvious weapon nearby. Either whoever killed him used his fists, or stomped him with his boots, or carried off the club he used."

John gritted his teeth as the marshal gave a further detailed description of the condition of the corpse. Crudder found it hard to imagine anyone could be so cruel.

"Was there any evidence to suggest Granger was the murderer?" asked John.

"Only the fact that Granger was the only one anyone ever considered who could do something so cruel. In the time Granger lived here, he was in numerous fights. Every time he had to be pulled off his victim. He would keep beating or stomping the other feller. I've never seen anyone who enjoyed bringing pain to others like Granger. But I've left out the worst murder I've ever heard of."

"Go ahead, Marshal. I guess I need to hear it all."

"John, this is hard for me to repeat. But about six months ago, the spinster schoolteacher, Jane Downey, was found murdered. She lived about two miles outside of town." The marshal paused and put his mug to his mouth. John watched him drink about half his beer before he continued.

"Anyway, I don't even like to think about what he did to her before he murdered her. It had to be Granger because no one else would do something as cruel as he did to poor ol' Miss Downey." The marshal looked down at his empty beer glass, his face frozen as he worked up the courage to add the rest of the story.

"He tied her hands behind her with wire and also tied her feet, but…" his voice trailed off as he contemplated how to tell the rest.

"John, he crammed a stick of dynamite down her throat and lit it. She…she…John, I've never seen anything like it."

Crudder sat stunned with what he had heard. He had seen many cruel people in his lifetime but the worst wasn't anywhere close to the cruelty of Granger. No wonder he was called The Butcher. John slowly sipped his beer and watched the marshal. It appeared Brodey was in pain from the memory of what he had witnessed.

"Marshal, I'm mighty sorry you had to see that. It must have been horrific. Do you know where Granger lived before he came to Kerrville?"

Brodey wrinkled his brow and thought about John's question. "Seems like he talked about Fredericksburg. He might have been from there."

"Marshal Williams said you believed Granger had some associates."

"Associates? John, you sound more like a lawyer than a former marshal."

"You got me there. I do have a law degree but I've never set up practice as a lawyer. I was asked by the city council of Bandera to be their marshal and I agreed but I didn't stay there long. I'm just a rancher now."

"Seems like I heard about a lot of foolishness the Bandera town council was mixed up in."

This time it was John who paused as he thought about to respond to Brodey. He didn't want to say too much for fear the marshal would suspect his role in cleaning out the town.

"Yes, there was evidence they were involved in a number of evil doin's in and around Bandera."

"I remember now," said Brodey. "I heard the Midnight Marauder cleaned up the town. Big feller. Bigger than me, I heard."

"That's what I heard as well," said John. He was grateful that the early descriptions of the Midnight Marauder didn't come close to describing someone of John's small stature. "Anyway, I was asking if Granger hung around with any other people."

"Associates, you called 'em," said the marshal with a smile on his face. "Yeah, I guess there were a few guys he hung out with. There was Skyler and Morgan. In fact, I think they showed up in town about the same time as Granger. And there was one other feller he used to talk to. It was an odd name. I can't seem to recall it. Hey, Willie, can you come over here for a minute?"

Wild Willie walked over to the table carrying two more beers. "Have a seat with us for a bit, will you, Willie?" asked the marshal.

"This here's John Crudder. He used to be the marshal in Bandera."

"Pleased to meet you, Marshal," said Willie.

"And I'm pleased to meet you as well. But it's just John. I'm no longer a marshal."

"Willie, I was just tellin' John here about Granger. I know he used to spend time with Morgan and Skyler. But what was the name of that other feller he'd sometimes be with?"

"You mean Quentin?" asked Willie.

"That's it," said the marshal. "Quentin. I don't think I've seen any of them in town since Granger robbed the bank."

"Marshal," said Willie, "I'd always assumed those three were in on the robbery with Granger."

"I never gave it no thought," said the marshal. "But it does make sense. The other three wore bandanas over their faces. The people in the bank didn't have much of a description of the other three. They focused primarily on Granger and over the senseless way he killed the bank clerk."

"Willie did Granger and those other three come in here much?" asked John.

"No, not much at all. I wouldn't serve 'em more than three drinks. After that I think people have had enough. They knew the rules here. At first they tried to force me into givin' them a bottle and lettin' 'em drink all they wanted. But they found out I kept a shotgun behind the bar. When we came to an understanding of how things were gonna go around here, they found it easier to just go somewhere else for their drinkin'."

John dropped a silver dollar on the table and stood up. "Well, gentlemen, I appreciate the information and I enjoyed the company. I wonder if you could tell me where I could get a beefsteak and a room for the evening?"

"The best food in town is at the Fat Hen Café," Willie said. "And there's a hotel right next door." Brodey nodded in agreement.

"I guess chicken will do," said Crudder. "Do you reckon they sell steaks?"

Willie and Brodey looked at each other and laughed.

"All they sell is beef," said the marshal. "The 'Fat Hen' refers to the owner and cook. Her late husband always referred to her as a Fat Hen. She misses him so much that she named her place so she can hear people talk about the Fat Hen every day."

John laughed and walked outside and untied Midnight. He had spotted the livery stable on the way into town. John swung up and let Midnight trot down to the livery. He unsaddled the stallion, paid the stableman for a bucket of oats, some hay, and a stall. Retrieving his dandy brush from his saddlebag, he spent the next half hour grooming his horse. When he finished, he walked to the hotel, registered, and paid for one night's lodging. Then he went next door to the Fat Hen.

The waitress introduced herself as Molly and asked what he wanted to eat. She was a small woman who looked to be about fifty years old. Her hair was thinning on top and was swept up into a bun that had a pencil sticking out of it. Her cheeks were rosy and her eyes were continuously in a squint. She had a small chin with generous amounts of skin from her chin to her neck.

"Pleased to meet you, Molly. What would you recommend?"

"Well, the meatloaf is good and so are the meatballs. But I think we make the best steak in town."

"You sold me on the steak. Could I get that with some fried potatoes?

"Sure can, hon. Would you like some coffee with that?" Molly took the pencil from her hair and made some scratches on the pad of paper she carried.

"I guess so. That sounds fine."

"How do you want your steak cooked, hon?"

"Medium rare would be good."

Molly smiled and then shouted at the kitchen. "Hey, Fat Hen. Make one bloody with taters." Molly walked to the coffee pot and returned with a cup for John. She gave him a wink as she placed the coffee on the table and turned to go back into the kitchen.

John smiled to himself as he thought about the forward waitress. As he waited for his food, he contemplated his next move. It made the most sense for him to head to Fredericksburg the next day. Maybe he could learn more about Granger and the three men he traveled with.

Roy Clinton

CHAPTER 4

The Road to Boerne, Texas

Granger woke up as Skyler was building up the campfire to make coffee. "What're you doing up so early?"

"No call to be gruff with me, Granger," said Skyler. "I wanted some coffee so I need to the fire going first. Is that all right with you?"

Granger huffed and turned over to try to go back to sleep. But the noise Skyler was making meant sleep was over for the day. Granger rolled up his bedroll and attached it to his saddle.

"Well if you're gonna make coffee, get on with it. I'm thirsty."

"Hold your horses," said Skyler. "It'll be ready directly."

Morgan woke up and stretched. "What's all the yellin' about?"

"No one's yellin' around here 'cept you and your brother," said Granger. "Someone wake up Quentin."

"I'm awake," said Quentin as he sat up and rubbed sleep from his eyes. "No one can sleep with all the racket goin' on. Why does everybody have to be so loud?"

Granger sneered and let out a laugh. "If I can't sleep, then ain't nobody else gonna sleep."

Skyler shook his head and added coffee to the water boiling in the pot. He grabbed a skillet and set it on a flat rock right at the edge of the fire. "Who's got the bacon?"

"I've got some," said Quentin who then went to his saddlebag and pulled out a small sack with about a half pound of bacon. He cut off a chunk with the knife he wore in the scabbard at his waist.

"I hope you cleaned that off before you cut the bacon," said Morgan. "The last time I saw you use that you were guttin' a squirrel."

"Don't you worry about it. I always wipe it off."

Morgan just shook his head. He didn't want to even think about all Quentin had done with the knife.

"Coffee's ready," said Skyler. Each man got up and filled his own cup.

"Granger, how much gold do we have?" asked Quentin.

"The old farmer said there was five hundred Double Eagles. That's two hundred for me," said Granger, "And a hundred for each of you."

"Why don't we get as much as you?" asked Quentin.

"Because you're not the boss," said Granger. "I am. You never even heard of the gold and wouldn't have any if it weren't for me. The way I see it, you have a hundred more now than you had before."

"When do we divide it up?" asked Morgan.

"Right after breakfast," said Granger. "I want me somethin' to eat first."

"Well, come and get it," said Skyler. "The bacon's done."

"Where're the biscuits?" asked Quentin.

"You ate the last of them yesterday," said Granger. "I watched you eat several of 'em as we were ridin'."

"I was hungry," said Quentin. "It didn't hurt for me to eat the biscuits. We can get more when we go into Boerne." Granger started laughing. "Why are you laughin'? All I did was eat some biscuits."

"I'm not laughing at you. I was just thinking of that old man and old woman back in Bandera. Did you hear him scream? I'll bet Jackson thought he could pull that poor farmer act on me and it would work. But I heard about him when I was a boy. Everyone knew he had lots of money."

"I'm glad you knew about it," said Morgan.

"And didn't he make some noise when I shot his wife," said Granger.

"He shor did," said Skyler. "You showed him good. But I didn't understand why you blew up their house."

"'Cause I just like the sound dynamite makes when it explodes."

Morgan and Skyler exchanged a look. They had seen the cruelty of Granger for years. While they didn't mind killing someone when they saw the need, they didn't see any reason to kill just for the sake of killing and destruction for no good reason.

"Well, they won't be around to spend any of their money

anyway," said Quentin. "It just ain't right for that old man and woman to have so much gold. We did the right thing relievin' 'em of it."

Granger laughed again. "You got that right. Gather round men. Let's split up the gold." Granger got both of his saddlebags and emptied them on the ground. He counted out one hundred coins in a pile and then repeated it in two other piles. Then he counted out two hundred coins for himself. He was left with three gold pieces. "Here you go. There was three more in the cookie jar. You get one each."

"Where do we go from here?" asked Morgan.

"I think it's like Quentin said. We need to go into Boerne and load up with supplies. Are any of you wanted in Boerne?" The men looked at each other and shook their heads. "Good. So, when we get through eatin', let's ride in and get what we need. But listen, men. We must keep it quiet. We can't afford for anyone to take notice of us. We need to keep it down for a few weeks. I'm sure the marshal in Bandera is lookin' for us."

"What good does it do to have money to spend if we can't live it up?" asked Skyler.

"Just get yourself a bottle in Boerne and you can party on the trail," said Granger.

"And what am I supposed to do for a woman?" asked Skyler.

"Just wait," said Granger. "I've got another job for us."

"Where are we goin' now?" asked Quentin.

"There's a stagecoach station outside of Fredericksburg," said Granger. "There is nothing anywhere around it and the stage always carries a strongbox. I've seen it unloaded many times when I lived in Fredericksburg."

"Are you crazy?" Quentin couldn't believe what he was hearing. "You're wanted for murder there. They'll be looking for you. For all of us."

"What'd you call me?" Granger growled as he turned slowly and sneered at Quentin.

"I just meant it's dangerous to go back there since people are looking for us there," offered Quentin in as soothing a voice as possible.

"We're not goin' to Fredericksburg," said Granger. "When we leave Boerne, we'll stay off the road and head due north. We shouldn't run into anyone before we get to the stage stop. And Quentin, we're gonna need the dynamite you're carrying in your saddlebags."

Quentin didn't like what he was hearing. He thought it was trouble to go back to where they had committed crimes in the past. It would be better, he thought, to go somewhere they had not been. But he also knew better than to argue with Granger. Granger was crazy. He knew that was true and so did Skyler and Morgan.

Roy Clinton

CHAPTER 5

Bandera, Texas

Slim sat on the porch of the home of his daughter Charlotte and son-in-law John Crudder. Claire was sitting on his knee and cradled in his left arm and Cora was on his right. They were almost too big for him to have both girls in his arms at once. Slim treasured these moments when he had some grandpa time.

He heard Charlotte stirring inside. "Morning, Daddy."

"Good mornin' dear."

"I'll make us some coffee and then I'll come right out and join you."

"Coffee would be good, thanks."

"I want some coffee," said Claire.

"Me too," said Cora. "I want some coffee. Mommy, we want coffee."

Charlotte giggled from the kitchen. "Girls, you don't like coffee. You don't even know what it tastes like."

"Yes, we do," said Cora.

"Grandpa lets us drink coffee," said Claire.

"All right, girls," said Slim. "I thought you said that was gonna be our secret."

"Mommy," said Cora. "Don't tell anyone. That's a secret."

"Keep our secret, Mommy," said Claire.

Charlotte came out wearing a big grin and set a mug of coffee for Slim on the side table. "Well, Grandpa, I guess you better go make the girls some coffee."

"Yea!" said Claire. "Remember I like sugar."

"And I like milk," said Cora.

"As I recall," Slim said, "you both like milk and sugar and a little coffee."

Slim went into the kitchen and pulled out some child-size mugs he had carved for the girls. He poured a little coffee and a lot of milk and sugar in each. After carefully mixing each and testing to make sure their drinks were not too hot, he carried them to the porch and set them beside his own mug.

"Come and get it girls," said Slim.

"So just how long have you been feeding my daughters coffee, Daddy?"

Slim dipped his head and frowned. "I didn't mean any harm. There's just a little coffee in their cups."

Charlotte laughed. "I'm not mad. I think it's cute."

"Whew! I thought I was in trouble."

"There's not much you can do to get in trouble," said Charlotte.

As they were talking, Richie, Charlotte's half-brother, arrived.

"Hey, when is breakfast gonna be ready?"

"Come take a seat, son. We're just havin' coffee now. Can I get you a cup?

"I'll get it, Pa," said Richie.

"Well," said Charlotte, "I think I need to get some breakfast going before there's a mutiny. How do pancakes sound?"

"Yea," said Cora, "I love pancakes."

"Me too," said Claire.

"That makes three," said Slim.

Richie came out to the porch with his coffee. "Pancakes sound great to me. I'll help you, Sis. I'm gettin' pretty good in the kitchen."

"I can use the help. Richie, go out to the spring house and bring in some sausage. Then you can be in charge of cooking it while I make the pancakes."

Richie ran over to the spring house which was located about halfway between Charlotte's house and the one where Slim and Richie lived. He ran back with the sausage and quickly shaped several patties and put them in the frying pan and placed them at the back of the stove.

Charlotte mixed up the batter and put another frying pan on the front of the stove. After testing the temperature with a few drops of dancing water, she started the first pancakes.

"Daddy, you and the girls get to set the table for us."

"I'll help," said Cora.

"Me too," said Claire.

"All right, Cora," directed Slim. "You get the forks and Claire, you get the knives. How many knives do we need?

Claire started counting people. "Four?"

"Cora, what do you think?" asked Slim. "How many forks do we need?"

Cora counted the people in the kitchen. "Five?"

"Well, let's see if there are four of us or if there's five." Slim said, "Your mommy is one. Richie is two. Cora, what number are you?"

"Three."

"And Claire, what number are you?"

"Four."

"So, I guess that's what we need," said Slim. It looks like we need four forks and four knives. Is that right? Did I forget anyone?"

Claire and Cora looked at each other with a puzzled look. Richie tried to get their attention. "Psst!" The girls looked at him. He pointed at Slim.

"Five," the girls said in unison.

"Oh, that's right. There's five of us," said Slim." Slim supervised the table setting and then got the girls in their chairs, elevated by small wooden boxes so they could reach the table. Richie served the sausage and Charlotte served up the pancakes.

"Whose turn is it to say grace?"

"Daddy's," the girls replied together.

"That's right," said Charlotte. "But Daddy's not here. So, whose turn is it next?"

"Richie's," replied both girls and they pointed across the table.

"I'll say it," said Richie as everyone joined hands and bowed their heads. "Lord, we thank you for the food you provide. We pray that you will bless it to the nourishment of our bodies. And bless John wherever he is and keep him safe. Amen."

Everyone responded with their own amen and started spreading butter and syrup on the pancakes. Slim got up and refilled the coffee cups. Compliments were given to Richie and Charlotte for the meal.

"Daddy, how long do you think John will be gone?"

"I'm not sure. Knowin' John, he's not gonna be content with just goin' to Kerrville. There's no telling where all he'll be goin'. I doubt he'll come home until he's found what he's lookin' for and before he had tended to what needs tendin' to."

"I know you're right, Daddy. It just always makes me nervous when he is away."

"John can handle himself," said Slim. "I know you know that. But what you also need to know is that he's not gonna take any unnecessary risks. He'll come home to all of us just as soon as he can."

Roy Clinton

CHAPTER 6

Kerrville, Texas

John woke up before sunrise, as was his practice. But when he was on the trail as the Midnight Marauder, he always got up extra early. He checked out of the hotel and went next door to the Fat Hen Café. To his surprise, Molly was working. He looked through to the kitchen and thought he saw the same woman cooking.

"Well, hon, you're back," said Molly as she brought him a cup of coffee and gave him a little wink. "What can I get for you?"

"I think I'd like a couple of scrambled eggs and some sausage," John said. "You wouldn't have any biscuits and gravy, would you?"

"Of course, we do, hon. And breakfast always comes with some fried taters."

"That sounds fine, Molly. And if it's not too much trouble, I'd also like some orange juice."

"Too much trouble? Well, will you listen to that? We don't

never have anyone in here with such good manners. Most don't care how much trouble something is. They just want what they want and they want it fast."

* * *

After breakfast, Crudder went to the livery and saddled Midnight. The sun would not be up for another hour but there was light on the eastern horizon. Midnight wanted to run but John held him back to a gentle lope until the sun was fully up. As dawn broke, John leaned forward ever so slightly and relaxed his hold on the reins. Midnight immediately went into a gallop. John smiled to himself and let his amazing horse run for about ten minutes. Reining Midnight back to a trot, John knew he would be in Fredericksburg by midmorning.

* * *

About an hour before he was to arrive in Fredericksburg, John passed the entrance to a horse ranch. The sign under an arched entrance said Morris Ranch. A small town was growing up outside the ranch. John stopped Midnight at a watering trough and swung down.

"Howdy, mister," shouted an old man who came over to pet Midnight. "Mighty fine animal you have here. Did you buy him from Morris?"

"No, sir. I bought him in New York. Looks like this ranch has a big horse operation."

"It's the biggest that we know of. Francis Morris owns twenty-three thousand acres. He raises thoroughbreds on it. This here horse of yours looks like a thoroughbred. Is he?"

"You have a good eye. Yes indeed, he's a thoroughbred. Any idea where I can find Mr. Morris?"

"I reckon you can find him at the house just through the arch. If he's not there, they'll know where to find him."

John thanked him and rode Midnight up to the sprawling house and swung down. As Crudder walked onto the porch, he noticed someone coming out of the nearby barn. He changed directions and led Midnight over to the barn.

"Howdy," said John to the hand coming out of the barn.

"Mornin'," came the reply.

"I wonder if I could buy a little feed for my horse," said John.

"Mighty fine animal you have there. Name's Morris. Francis Morris. You can just turn him into one of the empty stalls and let him eat his fill. No charge."

Francis Morris appeared to be in his mid-forties. He was a small man, only about three inches taller than John. His tanned and leathery skin spoke of the many hours he had spent in the sun. He had a wispy black beard and long hair that covered his ears and flowed down his back. Morris walked with a limp John surmised came as a result from being thrown from one of his thoroughbreds.

"Thanks, Mr. Morris. My name's John Crudder."

"As I was sayin', you have a mighty fine stallion, Mr. Crudder. I don't suppose you have papers on him, do ya?"

"I do, but he's not for sale."

"Who's talking about buying?" replied Morris. "I was thinking of seeing if you wanted to have him stand stud. Where did you get him?"

"I bought him at auction at Union Course in New York City."

"I know the track well," said Morris. "It's over in Queens. I moved here from New York and purchased some of my mares and a couple of fillies at the racetrack."

John looked around the barn and was amazed at what he saw. There were stalls for at least twenty horses. The walls of the stalls were barred to keep the high-strung animals safe from each other. At one end of the barn was a tack room filled with beautiful saddles and bridles. He noted the resemblance to stables at the track in New York.

"How about it, Mr. Crudder? Would you be interested in your horse standin' stud? I pay top dollar."

"I appreciate the offer, Mr. Morris. But I'm not going to be around here long. I'm on my way to Fredericksburg."

"Whatcha gonna do there? You lookin' for a job? I can always use another good hand."

"Thank you kindly, but I'm just looking for a man and thought I could find out more about him in Fredericksburg."

"What's his name?" asked Morris. "Maybe I know him."

"His name is Granger. I'm not sure what his first name is but people call him Butch."

The color drained from Morris's face as he stared Crudder. "I don't reckon he's a friend of yours, is he?"

"No, he's not. I've never met him."

"I'm glad to hear that. Granger is the scum of the earth."

"From what I have found out about him, I tend to agree," said Crudder. "Any idea where I could find him?"

"No, and I don't ever want to see him again," said Morris. "He killed one of my best stallions and stole three mares."

"When did this happen?"

Morris paused for a few seconds. "I think it was nigh on to three years ago. I had two no-account brothers workin' here. I was gonna fire 'em and I wish I had. If I'd fired 'em when I was thinkin' about it, I probably never would've met Granger."

"What happened, Mr. Morris?"

"Granger met the brothers in Fredericksburg. They decided to steal some horses from me. I caught 'em comin' out of this barn with the horses and I yelled at them to stop. Granger just smiled at me and pulled his gun. I thought he was gonna shoot me but he went over to a stallion and shot him in the head. If I would've had my gun, I would have killed him right then."

"I'm glad you didn't have a gun, Mr. Morris. From what I've learned about Granger, he would not have hesitated to have killed you if you tried to stop him."

"He had no call to shoot my horse. That stallion was important to my breedin' operation. I could have stood to lose the mares but the loss of the stallion has made it mighty difficult on me. That's why I was interested in your horse standin' stud."

"I'm sorry, Mr. Morris," said Crudder. "I have to find Granger. He murdered an elderly couple in Bandera. He has also killed people in other cities. I want to see him brought to justice. By the way, the brothers that worked here. Were their names Morgan and Skyler?"

"That's them."

"I hear they travel with another man named Quentin. Was he with them?"

"No, I've never heard of him. But if he's travelin' with Granger, then I'm sure he's also one of the devil's henchmen."

John extended his hand. "Mr. Morris, thanks for feedin' my horse. And thanks for the information about Granger. I better get started if I'm gonna make Fredericksburg by noon."

"I hope you catch 'em, young man. And I hope you can keep 'em from hurtin' anybody else."

"Thanks, Mr. Morris. I hope so, too.

CHAPTER 7

Bandera, Texas

Marshal Williams," shouted the telegraph operator as he was approaching the marshal's office. Clem got up and walked to the door. "I just got a telegram for you from the Texas Rangers. I wanted you to see it as soon as possible."

Marshal Williams
Bandera, Texas

The following is a current list of warrants for Granger. San Antonio, murder; Austin, murder; Kerrville, murder and bank robbery; Fredericksburg, horse theft, murder; Bandera, murder, and other crimes. If apprehended, prisoner to go to San Antonio first for trial.

Captain Jessup
Texas Rangers, Austin

Clem looked up to thank the telegraph clerk but found he had already left. He thought Slim should see the message so he mounted up and headed out to the H&F. He rode up to Slim's house and shouted for Slim. Owen came out of the barn.

"Howdy, Marshal," said Owen. "He's not here. I'll bet he's over at Crudder's place."

"Thanks, Owen." Williams wheeled his horse around and trotted across the yard to the home John has built for Charlotte. Sure enough, Slim was sitting on the porch playing with his granddaughters.

"Mornin', Mayor," said Williams.

"Howdy, Marshal. Come sit a spell. I'll get you a cup of coffee."

Clem swung down and had a seat on the porch. Immediately, Cora and Claire ran to great him. "Good mornin', ladies."

The little girls clung to Clem's legs and laughed.

"We're not ladies," said Cora.

"We're little girls," said Claire.

"Oh, that's right. I forgot." Slim arrived carrying two mugs of coffee.

"So, what's goin' on to get you out of the office so early in the mornin'?"

"I got this telegram and thought you'd want to see it."

Williams handed Slim the folded piece of paper. Slim read it slowly and then read it a second time. "I wish I knew where to contact John. He'd want this information."

"Any idea where he is now?" asked the marshal.

"No, I don't have a clue. I know he was goin' to Kerrville first. My guess is he left there this mornin' and headed out based on information he got there."

"I guess there's nothing we can do until we hear from him," said the marshal.

"I guess not," responded Slim. "We could send messages on ahead of him to several towns in hopes he'll check in at one of them. But he'll not likely be lookin' for a message since we don't know where he is travelin'. Tell you what, Clem. When you get back to town, address telegrams to John and send them to Kerrville, Fredericksburg, and Austin. Copy what the Texas Rangers said and tell him to be careful.

"That sounds like a good plan, Slim. I'll head back to town and send them now."

Roy Clinton

CHAPTER 8

Fredericksburg, Texas

Having never been to Fredericksburg, John was not sure what to expect. What he didn't anticipate was the strong German influence. As he rode through town, he noted several businesses with German-sounding names.

The thing that struck him most was the width of Main Street. John guessed it was every bit as wide as Fifth Avenue in New York City. He stopped at an eating establishment named Fraulein Hilda's Café, swung down and tied Midnight to the hitching rail. Inside, he asked the waitress what was good.

"Vell, I vould say the Bratwurst or the viener schnitzel are the best."

John realized he had not had any German food since he was in Europe for graduate school. "I think I'll have the wiener schnitzel and some potato pancakes." The waitress smiled and disappeared into the kitchen. In just a few minutes she reappeared with his meal. The food was wonderful. He made a mental note to ask Charlotte to try to duplicate the meal when he got home.

Crudder finished eating and walked to the telegraph office to tell Charlotte and Slim where he was. As he dictated the message, the telegraph operator stopped writing and told him he had received a message for him earlier that morning. John read the telegram and then hurriedly wrote out another message.

Slim Hanson
Bandera, Texas

Got your message. All is well. Give my love to Charlotte. Will check in every few days.

John Crudder
Fredericksburg, Texas

John paid the operator and waited to verify the message had been sent and then walked over to the marshal's office.

"Howdy, Marshal," John said as he removed his hat and entered the office. The marshal was sitting at his desk but looked up and tipped his hat back on his head.

"Afternoon," replied the marshal. "What can I do for you? You look like a stranger to these parts."

"I am, Marshal. My name's John Crudder. I live in Bandera and used to be the marshal there." John had learned he got further with law officers if he introduced himself as a former marshal.

"Pleased to meet you, John. Name's Junior Wilson. You must be here lookin' for someone."

"Why do you say that?" asked Crudder.

"Now John, you know it's always easy to spot a lawman—even an ex lawman. And for you to be here to see me, it just makes sense you'd be lookin' for someone."

John smiled as he recognized the truth of the marshal's statement. "You're right, Marshal. I'm here to find out what I can about Butch Granger."

The marshal shook his head slowly. "I had hoped I wouldn't hear that name again. I would say that man's a snake but that would be an insult to reptiles. Granger is the most heartless man I've ever known. I'm still findin' out about things he did while he was here."

John nodded his head in agreement. "I got a telegram saying he was wanted for murder here."

"That's right," said Marshal Wilson. "I've never seen anything like what he did to that couple." Junior paused and looked off into the distance before continuing. "Pops and Granny Thomas never did nothin' to no one. Granger had no right to kill 'em. And he didn't just kill 'em. He tortured 'em."

John waited for the marshal to continue when he realized that he wasn't going to speak any more without prompting. "Marshal, can you tell me what he did?"

"John, it was the worst thing I'd ever seen. He took Pops and Granny out to their barn and he strung up Pops to a rafter by his thumbs and beat him. Doc said Pops' legs were broken all to pieces. Pops' thumbs—his thumbs—were pulled completely off." The marshal paused and shook his head. "Then Granger put wire around Pops' hands and he trussed him up to the rafter.

"And Granny—she was stomped. Her hands and feet were completely destroyed. When my deputy and I investigated the murder scene, we figured Granger strung up Pops so he had to watch when he beat up Granny. John, he finally killed her by stomping her in the head. It was the most gruesome thing I've ever seen."

John could feel his face burning and anger rose within him. He was more determined than ever to make sure Granger paid for his crimes.

"How did you know it was Granger that did it?"

"Well there were several things that pointed to Granger. Pops' cow dogs were shot dead. One of them was gutted with a shovel. And all the livestock were killed. Granger put a bullet in all of Pops' horses and cattle. The only one in Fredericksburg who's ever been cruel to animals is Granger. I've had several of his neighbors say Granger killed their dogs or cats."

"How long did Granger live here?"

The marshal scratched his chin. "I think it must have been about a year. Maybe longer. But he's been gone for at least four years. And I've not heard anything from him since he left here."

"Did he have any accomplices?"

"There was a man named Quentin he used to ride with. Quentin was just about as mean as Granger. He was always fast with his gun or a knife. Quentin killed a man in a barfight. No charges were brought 'cause others in the bar said the other man drew first. But Quentin had baited the man into drawing. The man he killed was just an old farmer who wasn't much of a gun hand."

"There are some brothers named Morgan and Skyler who ride with Granger. Did they ever come around here?

"Yes, they've been in and out of here for years," said the marshal. "But I've never seen 'em with Granger. They were just here about a month ago."

John perked up. "Do you know where they went?"

The marshal shook his head. "Don't rightly know. They were in a hurry when they left. Several businesses were broken into during the night. We don't know for certain who did it but Morgan and Skyler visited each business two days before the burglaries."

"But there wasn't any sign of Granger?" asked John.

"No, there's no way he was in town or I would have heard."

"What that says to me is that Granger is close by, or at least he was a month ago when you saw Morgan and Skyler."

"You're probably right about that. I do have one request," said Marshal Wilson. "If you find any of the bunch, I wish you'd bring 'em back here to stand trial."

"I know you'd like that, Marshal. But the Texas Rangers have already ordered that Granger has to stand trial in San Anton first."

Nodding his head, the marshal said, "I guess that's just as well. We'll get to try Granger here eventually—that is if they don't hang him first. And the other three in his gang need to stand trial here as well."

"Thanks for your help, Marshal," said Crudder. "I'll probably stay here for the rest of the day and then I'll head out."

"Which way are you headed?"

"I haven't decided yet."

"Well if you go east, you'll get to the stage stop in Stonewall. The stage from there was due here at noon but it's overdue. Probably nothin' to it. It's run late before. But if you go that way, I'd be obliged if you'd keep an eye out for it."

"Tell you what, Marshal. I didn't have any other plans for this afternoon so I think I'll ride out that way. About how far is the stage station?"

"It's about fifteen miles more or less."

"I've never heard of Stonewall before," said Crudder."

"No reason you should," said the marshal. "Nothing much there but the stage stop. Named it after Stonewall Jackson. Don't rightly know why. Far as I know, he was never in these parts."

"Thanks again, Marshal. Maybe I'll see you again."

"Good luck to you, John. I shor hope you catch up with Granger."

CHAPTER 9

Stonewall, Texas

I'm tired of ridin'," Skyler groused. "Why'd we have to leave so early this morning? And when are we gonna get there?"

"Quit your complainin'," growled Granger. "We'll get there when we get there."

"I'm recognizin' where we are," said Morgan. "Looks like we're just an hour or so from Stonewall. Is that where we're goin'?"

"It is. And you're right, we should be there in about an hour."

"Now I remember," said Skyler. "There's a general store there. I didn't know it was also a stage stop."

"The stagecoach station is the back part of the store," added Granger. "Some old man and woman run the place. I'll bet we can get a good meal while we're there."

"That would suit me fine," said Quentin. "I'm shor tired of bacon and jerky. What time does the stage get there?"

"Probably around mid-morning," said Granger. "Then it will take about two hours to get to Fredericksburg, arriving around noon. Now you know why we had to leave so early this mornin'."

The gang continued riding and soon came to a clearing. They stopped at the edge of the clearing and waited for Granger to give direction.

"On the far side of the clearing is the store and stage stop," said Granger. "It don't look like the stage has gotten there yet." They continued riding in a trot until they got to the store.

All four swung down and tied their horses to the hitching rail. As they went into the store, the door slammed against the frame. An old couple emerged from the back of the store. They had smiles on their faces until they saw the riders.

"Hello, gentlemen," said the old man. "I thought the stage was here. It's due here soon."

"We're not on the stage but we shor are hungry," said Granger.

"Come on in," said the old woman. "I've about got breakfast ready for the stage and I've cooked plenty. Y'all come on in and take a seat in the back. If you want to wash up, there's a pump and basin out back."

"I reckon we'll pass on washin' up, ma'am," said Granger as he took off his hat. He looked at the other men and said, "This ain't no barn. You men take off your hats."

The three obliged and followed Granger to the back of the store. It opened into another room that had several bunks built into the side walls. There were four long tables in the middle of the room with each surrounded by a combination of benches and chairs. All four sat at a table and hung their hats over the tops of the ladder-back chairs.

In a few minutes, platters of scrambled eggs, potatoes, and biscuits were brought to the table. The men ate hungrily, devouring all the food in front of them. Their host made several trips by their table refilling their coffee mugs.

When they had eaten their fill, they pushed their chairs back from the table. Granger caught the eyes of the other men; a silent communication being exchanged.

"Ma'am," said Granger, "that was mighty fine cookin'. Skyler, why don't you go find her husband and pay him for the meal."

"He's just up in the general store," offered the woman.

"Skyler, you take care of him," said Granger. "Morgan, I want you to pay this lady for the nice meal she made for us."

As Morgan pulled his gun, a shot was heard from the other room. The old woman let out a scream and put her hands to her face. Morgan's shot went through both of her hands and into her skull. She dropped instantly to the floor.

"Quentin," Granger ordered, "move the horses around back and bring in a stick of dynamite. Skyler and Morgan, pull the bodies out back. I don't want 'em clutterin' up things."

After each man had accomplished his task, they gathered around Granger and waited for further instructions.

"When the stage gets here," Granger said, "I'll go out and stand in front of the horses. The driver and his guard will be paying attention to me. Quentin, I want you to stay in here and light the dynamite. Let the fuse burn down low, then come out the door and throw it in the stage. When I see you coming out, I'll kill the guard and the driver. After you hear the explosion, Skyler and Morgan, I want you to make sure all the passengers are dead. If they're not, take care of 'em. Then drag 'em out and see what loot they're carryin'."

"What about the strongbox?" asked Quentin.

Granger turned toward him and sneered. "Does it sound like I'm through? Do you think since we came here for the strongbox, I would leave it?"

"I'm sorry, Granger," said Quentin. "I was just wonderin' if you wanted me to get it down."

"That's exactly what I want you to do. And Skyler and Morgan, when you've finished with the passengers, I want you to see if you can find where these old folks keep their money. They've got to have a lot of it. They've had this store and stage stop for a long time."

As he finished his instructions, the sound of the arriving stage filled the room. Quentin struck a match and held it near the stick of dynamite. Granger went outside and stood in front of the horses as the guard approached.

"Howdy," said Granger. "Looks like y'all are runnin' a bit late."

"Where's old man Thornton?" asked the guard.

"Oh, he'll be out directly."

Just then the door of the store opened. Quentin threw the stick of dynamite inside the stage and ran back inside. As the guard turned to see what was happening, Granger pulled his six-gun, killing him and then shot the driver.

After the explosion, the door to the store opened and the three outlaws came out to the stage. They opened the doors and started dragging mangled passengers out one by one. Skyler and Morgan each shot passengers they judged to still be alive. In all there were five dead passengers, one man, three women, and a baby.

Quentin threw down the strongbox and shot off the lock. It was filled with gold bars. Granger saw the bounty and whooped with joy. There was much more than he anticipated.

"This is gonna be more than we can carry for long," said Granger. "We'll need to ride a ways and then bury it. We can come back and get it when we run out of Double Eagles and the law's not lookin' for us."

As the men searched the bodies, Granger walked up to the horses that were hitched to the stage and shot each in the head. Skyler and Morgan looked at each other in horror. Quentin just shook his head. Then Granger went into the corral and killed the eight relief horses.

The men loaded their saddlebags with gold bars but there was still much more left in the strongbox.

"Go get some flour sacks," Granger ordered no one in particular. "Double 'em up and fill 'em up with the rest of the bars."

The men went about their tasks silently. Discarded flour covered the floor of the store and the area around the stage. With the gold loaded, they mounted their horses and struck out to the west.

Roy Clinton

CHAPTER 10

John set out for Stonewall, holding Midnight to a trot. He was in no hurry and knew he would use the time for thinking about his next move. John always thought best in the saddle.

"I'm sorry, boy, but you don't get to run now. I need to think so you can just take your time."

Midnight whinnied in response. John laughed as he reflected on how it always seemed like Midnight understood him. He rode for about an hour and a half before he saw the stage stop coming into view. From a distance he could tell the stage was still there.

Something was wrong but he couldn't tell what it was. Why would the stage be sitting in the road in front of the stage stop? Wouldn't the driver pull it to the side so the horses could be swapped out and the road wouldn't be blocked?

As he got closer, he felt sick to his stomach. The first thing he could make out were the four dead horses still hitched to the stage. As he got closer, he saw the driver and guard sitting atop the stage, both obviously dead.

Nothing could have prepared John for what he saw next. When

he got even with the horses he saw the badly mangled remains of the passengers. But what broke his heart was seeing the contorted body of the infant. Tears formed in his eyes but were quickly replaced with a greater anger than he had ever felt. He cursed under his breath.

John swung down and went inside to see what happened to the proprietors. He saw the store had been ransacked and the floor covered in flour. John made a mental note of it and walked out the back door. There he found the bodies of the old man and his wife. Over in the corral, he found eight more dead horses.

What kind of animal could do such things? Instantly he knew this was the work of Granger and his gang of outlaws. John bowed his head and said a silent prayer for those who had died at the hands of the evil men. He wanted to bury them but knew the best thing he could do was to get back to Fredericksburg just as soon as possible so the marshal could come and investigate.

He mounted Midnight and let out a yell as he gave the stallion his head. He was back in town in less than an hour.

CHAPTER 11

Fredericksburg, Texas

Crudder rode directly to the marshal's office. Once again, the marshal was not there so John went down to Wild Willie's Saloon. Sure enough, the marshal was there for his afternoon beer. But John wondered if perhaps that was just his other office.

Crudder waved away Willie indicating he was not there for a beer. Instead he went up to the marshal. "Wilson, I need to see you back at your office."

"Come have a beer first, John. There's no hurry." But John had already walked out of the saloon and was rapidly making his way to the marshal's office. "Why are you in such an all-fired hurry?" asked Wilson.

Wilson arrived at his office and was obviously perturbed that he had to put aside his afternoon recreation. "John, I thought you were gonna ride out to Stonewall."

"I've already been there, Marshal. You better take a seat 'cause today's noon stage is not coming in—ever!" As Wilson sat down at his desk, he adopted a much more serious look.

"All right, Crudder. You have me here. Now what's this all about?"

"Marshal, everyone is dead."

"What? What do you mean, everyone is dead?"

"I went to Stonewall, and I could see the stage sitting in the middle of the road in front of the stage station. As I got closer, I saw that all four horses that had been pulling the stage had been shot. They lay dead hooked to their harnesses. Then I saw the driver and shotgun rider were both dead, still sitting in the box. But Marshal, I also realized someone had dynamited the stage with the passengers still inside.

"I've never seen such a horrible sight. It was even worse than what I saw when Granger blew up the Jackson home in Bandera with Mrs. Jackson still inside. Marshal, the bodies were in pieces. They had been pulled out of the stage and it was evident that they had been robbed of anything valuable. There were three women and a man. But there was also a baby." John's eyes once again filled with tears as he contemplated the fact that the baby would never learn to walk, go to school, get married, or have children.

"Out back of the general store, I found the bodies of an elderly couple. I'm guessing they ran the store and the stage stop."

"That would have been old man Thornton and his wife," said Wilson. "They were among the kindest people I have ever met. They were always willin' to do anything for anybody."

"It looks like they fed the murderers before they were shot. There were four dirty plates at a table with four empty coffee cups," Crudder added. "And they weren't used by the stage passengers for they all died inside their stage."

"So, they got fed a meal and then just shot the old couple?"

"That's what it looks like to me, Marshal. Oh, and they also killed the horses that were in the corral. I think there was eight of them."

"Nothing like this has ever happened round here. Do you think it was Granger?"

"Everything points to it if you ask me," said Crudder. "There are four in the Granger gang that we know of, and there's evidence that four people ate breakfast just before the stage arrived. And don't forget Granger likes to kill animals. I've never come across any outlaw that did that."

"When do you think they were killed?"

"Well, you said the stage was due here at noon. It probably takes the stage two hours to get here from Stonewall. There was more breakfast waiting to be served to the passengers so I'm guessing with the breakfast and swappin' out the horses, they allow for about a one hour stop. Everyone on the stage was killed on the stage so that happened as soon as it arrived. I would guess this all took place around nine o'clock this mornin'."

Wilson looked at Crudder with surprise. "That sounds right to me, John. I can tell you've investigated crime scenes before."

"A few," replied John. "But Marshal, I think it's important for you to get out there before dark. I left everything just as I found it so you can conduct a proper investigation."

"I know you're right about that. If we hurry, we can make it before dark. Let me get my deputy and we'll get started."

"Marshal, you might want to line up several wagons to bring in the bodies and alert the undertaker to prepare to work through the night."

"Good idea," said Wilson. "I'll go by the lumberyard and the freight office and get them to send out wagons just as soon as they can. Do you think two will be enough?"

"I guess so. More might be better since there are eight adults and the baby."

"That's right," replied Wilson. "Three would be better. What about the dead horses?"

John found it curious that Wilson was looking to him to tell him how to do his job. "Well, Marshal, there's gonna have to be a powerful lot of digging done to bury those horses where they are. And there are so many of them, they'll need to be buried extra deep. By morning, you're gonna need a small army equipped with shovels to take care of digging the graves. I've never had to dig a grave for a horse but I did once for a steer. Three of us were digging and it still took us a couple of hours. Then with the graves dug, we'll need to hitch up other horses to drag them into the graves."

Wilson hung his head as he thought about the work that was ahead of him. He seemed immobilized with the weight of the tasks before him.

"I know," said John, "you're plannin' on gettin' a posse

together to track down Granger and the gang."

Wilson came to attention like that thought had just occurred to him. "But it's too late to do much lookin' today."

"I think you're right, Marshal. But you can get the word out that the posse will leave at first light and the diggin' crew also needs to get started then."

"Where am I gonna find enough men to do all that needs doin'?"

John's surprise got even greater as he realized the marshal had likely never had to gather a posse. "Well, Marshal, you might get word out at Wild Willie's and the other saloon that all men are needed first thing in the morning. Get the bartenders to give you the names of their customers. Tell them they'll either ride posse or dig graves for horses. Let 'em choose what they want to do."

"That's a good plan," said the marshal. "I'll go line up the wagons. Would you mind telling Willie what I want him to do? And then go to the other saloon and tell them you're there on my behalf."

"I'll be glad to, Marshal. I'll meet you back here in fifteen minutes so we can get started to Stonewall."

The marshal turned back to Crudder. "And if you see my deputy, tell him what's goin' on."

Wilson rode out to the lumberyard and freight office while John went over to Wild Willie's. Willie had seen John and the marshal together so he readily accepted the message John gave as coming directly from the marshal. The other saloon was a different story.

John went into the saloon and the first thing he noticed was the deputy marshal at the end of the bar. John wondered if the marshal and deputy did their drinking in different bars in order to keep watch on more of the town or because they just didn't like drinking together.

John approached the deputy. "Deputy, my name is John Crudder. I am here with a message from Marshal Wilson. He wants you to meet him back at the marshal's office right now." The bartender came over to take John's order.

"You want a beer, mister?"

"No, thank you," replied John. "The marshal sent me to tell you to take the name of every customer you have tonight and pass the word to them they're all to be at the marshal's office at first light. Some will be on a posse goin' after the people who murdered the stage passengers out at the Stonewall station. The rest will be doin' graveyard duty to bury the horses that were killed out there."

"Just who do you think you are, mister?" asked the bartender. "You little twerp, you can't come in here and give me orders on what I'm supposed to do. This is my business and I'll run it the way I want to run it."

The bartender stepped around the bar and reared back his fist intending to teach John a lesson. John side stepped the big man and landed two punches in the man's gut and two more to his jaw. The big man dropped instantly and was out cold. As he was dropping, the deputy pulled his six-gun, but John wrested it from his grip and turned it on him.

"Deputy, I really don't have time to put up with your foolishness. You better get down to the marshal's office now. I'll give you your gun back when you get there." John looked at the other men who were gathered around. "When the bartender comes to, remind him the marshal wants him to take the name of every customer who comes in tonight and every man is to show up at the marshal's office in the morning at first light."

Grudgingly, the deputy walked out of the saloon followed by John. They both swung up and trotted to the marshal's office. It was evident the deputy was both angry and embarrassed being bested by the small man on the big black horse.

The marshal was just arriving when John and the deputy rode up. John spoke first. "Marshal, one thing I didn't mention earlier is that we're gonna need the hardware store to open up in the morning so we can get shovels and pickaxes."

"I'll stop by there on our way out of town," said Wilson.

"Who is this little guy, Marshal?" asked the deputy. "I don't know who he is but all he's doin' is giving orders. I'm tired of lettin' him boss us around."

"Buford," said Wilson, "just shut up. I don't know why I put up with you. You don't have the sense enough to come in out of the rain. And I see Crudder's already had to take your gun away from you."

"Oh, I forgot," said Crudder as he handed the deputy his gun and extended his hand to shake. "No hard feelings?"

Buford took the gun but ignored Crudder's outstretched hand. "Buford," said Marshal Wilson, "you either shake Crudder's hand or turn in your badge." Buford stuck out his hand. John leaned over and shook it.

"I am glad to meet you, deputy," said John. "We've got a hard afternoon ahead of us."

Buford didn't say anything but kept a sour face as he watched the marshal go into the hardware store. When Wilson came out, he swung up, turned his horse to the south, and went into a trot. John and Buford followed. Before the road turned east toward Stonewall, John saw four wagons, each being pulled by teams of two, coming out of town. Wilson waved at the wagons and then said, "Let's go men. We need to make tracks for Stonewall."

The marshal's horse shot forward followed by Buford's. John signaled for Midnight to be patient and settle for following what would surely prove to be slower horses. The other horses were running in a gallop but Midnight was in a gentle lope and moved up beside the other horses. Wilson and Buford looked over at Midnight in awe.

It took about an hour to get to Stonewall. Marshal Wilson slowed his horse as the stage stop came into view. All three horses slowed to a walk and approached what looked more like a battlefield than a crime scene. As the dead horses came into view, Buford leaned over the side of his saddle and threw up the contents of his stomach and then continued to dry heave.

John swung down and tied Midnight as the marshal and deputy sat in their saddles surveying the damage. Finally, they swung down and tied their horses. Silence hung between them and they walked among the dead. John walked into the store and Wilson followed him. They walked through the store and John pointed out the table with what was left of the breakfast the gang had shared. John walked out the back door followed by the marshal.

Neither man spoke as the marshal knelt beside each body to get a closer look. He shook his head and stood up to follow John to the corral. Flies had gathered on the horses. There was a continual buzzing sound in the air. When they got back to the stagecoach, they found Buford bending over and throwing up by the corpses of the passengers.

"Dag nab it, Buford. Don't throw up there. Walk away from the bodies. You're contaminating the scene."

"I'm sorry, Marshal. I've just never seen anything like this. I don't think I'm cut out to be a deputy. I'm goin' back to town."

"Buford," said the marshal, "you may not be cut out to be a deputy and if you want to quit tomorrow then you can quit. But you're gonna stay here and help in the investigation. And then if you quit, you need to know you'll still be part of the posse I'm forming tomorrow. And if you refuse, I'll throw your no-account self in jail."

The marshal's strong words seemed to straighten Buford out. He started paying attention to what the marshal was doing and following him to try to see things from his point of view.

"I see they got into the strongbox," said Wilson.

"Marshal, do you have any idea what they were carryin'?" asked Crudder.

"Not yet. But any time they send a shotgun rider, that usually means they're carryin' gold. I'll find out from Wells Fargo in the mornin', but I think it's safe to say it was a shipment of gold."

"Marshal," Buford spoke up. "Why do you think there's flour spread all around? There is flour everywhere."

"That's a most curious thing," said the marshal. "They pretty well tore up everything inside. But it does look like they paid special attention to the flour. It looks like they were just trying to make a mess."

"I guess so," said Buford.

John walked around the area and stared at the ground. He was trying to find a pattern or a reason for the flour being strewed about.

"Marshal," said John. "If you're right about the strongbox holdin' gold, how much do you think the strongbox would weigh?"

"I don't know. I guess it could be close to a couple hundred pounds—maybe more."

"That's what I was thinkin'," said John. "And they probably still have the gold they stole from the old couple in Bandera they murdered."

The marshal's face brightened as he started following John's line of reasoning. "So, they wouldn't have had room in their saddlebags for that much gold. They could've used the flour sacks to carry the gold. Right?"

"That makes sense to me," John replied.

"But even puttin' the gold into flour sacks," Buford offered, "their horses couldn't carry that much weight."

"And I would bet they didn't have any pack animals," added John. "My guess is Granger decided to kill the horses before he thought through about how he was going to get away with the gold."

"Then what did they do with it?" asked Buford.

"That means the gold is still here some place."

"I think you're right, Marshal," said Crudder. "I'm guessin' they didn't go very far before they stopped to hide the gold with the intention of pickin' it up later."

"How will we ever find it?" asked Buford. "They could have put it anywhere around here."

Marshal Wilson and Crudder exchanged a look and a grin. "We follow the flour," said the marshal.

"That's right," said John. "Just like Hansel and Gretel followin' the bread crumbs, we'll follow the flour."

"Huh?" Buford scratched his head. "What are you talkin' about?"

"I think we mount up and each take a different direction and look for flour that has been spilled," said the marshal.

"I didn't see any flour on the road back to Fredericksburg," said John. "Why don't we start out the other way and see what we can find."

The three mounted up and spread out several feet between them and headed east. They had only gone a few feet when Buford yelled, "Look here. Flour everywhere!"

Wilson and Crudder rode over to see what Buford had found. Over the next few minutes they took their horses off the road and looked for more flour. They found many traces of it. Indeed, it was like following breadcrumbs. A couple of hundred yards off the road, they found an area where the ground had been freshly dug. It appeared someone had tried to disguise the digging by covering it with brush and a small pile of stones to mark the site.

John swung down and retrieved the short-handled shovel he always carried in his saddlebag. After ten minutes of digging, he unearthed several flour sacks filled with gold bars.

"Wow!" said Buford. "You were right, Crudder. Just like Hansel and Gretel."

"Buford," directed the marshal. "Go back to the stage and get one of the wagons. Bring it here and ask the men to load the bodies in the other wagons."

"Yes, sir." Buford rode hard back to the store and in a few minutes came back being followed by a wagon. The wagon driver climbed down to help the other three men load the gold. When it was loaded, they all went back to the murder site and helped load the bodies in the wagons. Marshal Wilson and Crudder transferred the contents of the flour sacks back to the strongbox and put the strongbox in the wagon.

The four wagons headed back to Fredericksburg. Buford rode with the gold. John pulled his saddle gun and loaned it to Buford as he provided protection. John and the marshal rode back to town to get things organized for the next day. They rode about as fast as they had on the way to Stonewall. The marshal's horse was struggling so John suggested that they take it a bit easier for the sake of the animals.

Back in town, Marshal Wilson and John went by both saloons to verify the bartenders were gathering names and passing word about the posse and grave duty. Wild Willie was onboard and had his list on the bar. Everyone there was aware of the tasks ahead of them the next morning.

They rode to the other end of town and entered the saloon. When they walked through the door, the bartender yelled, "What are you doin' back here? Marshal Wilson, this man came in here and picked a fight with me. He beat me up and knocked me out."

Wilson smiled, "Well, Harry, it looks like you outweigh Crudder by a hundred pounds and are more than a foot taller than he is. It don't seem likely he picked a fight with you."

"He did, Marshal. He came in here givin' me orders and I just came around the bar to find out more about what he was sayin' and that's when he beat me up."

There were snickers around the bar and the patrons recalled the one-sided fight they had witnessed a couple of hours earlier.

"So, Harry, where's the list you're supposed to be keeping for me?" asked the marshal.

"Marshal, I don't take orders from this little guy."

"He told you he was carryin' a message from me and you *will* take orders from me." The marshal turned toward the men at the bar. "I want all of you men at my office in the mornin'. Nine people have been murdered out at the Stonewall stage stop. Twelve horses have been slaughtered as well. I need every one of you, including you, Harry. You can either be on the posse or digging graves for the horses. You get to decide which you want to do. But all of you are required to be there. You'll all be paid a dollar a day for your work.

"Now, Harry, you start writin' down the names of everyone here. And anybody else that comes in, you tell 'em to see me at first light tomorrow and you bring the list of names with you. Anyone who doesn't appear will be fined. Any questions?"

There was some grumbling but most of the talk was about the grisly crime that had been committed. "I also need some of you men to volunteer to help the undertaker tonight. I'm sure he doesn't have nine coffins ready. How many of you men are good carpenters? You'll get extra pay for helping tonight." Several men raised their hands. "All right, you men go over and help the undertaker. Ruben, can you open the lumberyard so they can get materials for the coffins?"

"Sure thing, Marshal. I'll go unlock it right now."

"Thanks, Ruben. And keep an inventory of the supplies that are used. I'll make sure you get paid."

"I 'preciate that, Marshal."

Marshal Wilson and Crudder walked out of the saloon, mounted up and went to the marshal's office. Wilson put on a pot of coffee and the two men discussed the tasks ahead.

"John, where do you think Granger and the gang went?"

"Well, we know they didn't come back here. And they buried the gold out east of Stonewall. There are warrants out for them in Austin, San Anton, Kerrville, and Bandera."

"Then it seems most likely they're headed north," said the marshal. "What do you think?"

"That seems to make sense," said Crudder. "Most people would try to get as far away from where they committed crimes so I guess the most logical thing would be to look to the north. Maybe Llano or Mason."

"Yeah, they might even have gone on to San Angelo or Abilene, or maybe even Fort Worth or Dallas."

"That's a lot of ground to cover," said Crudder. "We're most likely to catch 'em if we try to track them just as soon as possible. I think you may well be right about the gang going north. But Granger is not normal in any way I've found yet. He's not gonna do the predictable."

"So, what are you sayin'?" asked the marshal.

"I'm just thinking that we have to look to the north like you were sayin' but we also need to realize he could be goin' back to some of the places he's been before."

"John, I can't afford to split up the posse."

"I know that, Marshal. I agree the posse should head out north. What I was thinkin' is that I might head over to Austin and then swing south."

"That's good thinkin'," said the marshal. "I'll deputize you so you can have the law behind you."

"Thanks, Marshal. But if it's all the same to you, I'd rather not carry a badge. I've found a badge sometimes slows me down. I need to be able to ride and move without regard to being concerned about some of the legal niceties."

The marshal arched his brows as he looked at John. "I'm not sure what to say. But I can see where you're comin' from. It is obvious you know how to handle yourself. Harry is no pushover and you quickly put him in his place. And you also disarmed Buford, though that boy is just a big idiot. But there's one other thing. When you were loading the sacks of gold, your shirt sleeve pulled up and I saw the scabbard on your right wrist. Are you any good with that thing?"

John was silent for a few moments. As far as he knew, no one had ever seen the dagger he carried on his forearm unless he had to use it. And he was quite sure even fewer knew of the twin daggers carried in scabbards on his back. "Well, I guess I do all right, Marshal. I can use it when I need to."

"It also appears to me you carry a knife or two down the back of your shirt."

The surprise showed on John's face as the marshal smiled. "Don't be shocked. I know I'm not nearly as good at investigatin' crimes as you are. You've proven that to me today. But I am observant. Several times when you bent forward, I noticed the outline of the daggers on your back."

John was stunned. "I'm not sure what to say. But you're right about one thing. You are observant."

"So, I'm guessin' there's much more to you than meets the eye. How'd you get so proficient with your fists and with daggers?"

"Marshal, it's a long story but I'm willin' to tell you since you asked. I grew up in New York City and, as you might imagine, I was picked on a lot since I'm so small. I was sent off to boardin' school and continued to suffer from the bullies at school.

"I joined the boxing team and got pretty good with my fists. Some of the boys on the team took me under their wings and showed me the fine art of what they called street fightin'. I found out there were a number of additional things I needed to learn if I was gonna defend myself outside the boxing ring."

"You must have learned 'em pretty well," said the marshal. "I don't think anyone has ever gotten the best of Harry."

"Then I went to law school 'cause I wanted to see people get justice. While there, I got introduced to Lady Justice, you know the statue of the blindfolded woman holding Scales of Justice? I wanted to spend my life helping balance the Scales of Justice for those who couldn't speak for themselves."

"So, did you ever practice law?"

"I've never set up a practice but I've done a bit of legal work." John wanted to say more about how he had become the Midnight Marauder to take care of the thieves and murderers who composed the Bandera town council. But he knew he needed to steer clear of that subject. Marshal Wilson had already proved to be a keen observer. Crudder couldn't risk saying much more.

"What about the daggers?" asked the marshal.

"When I came out west, I saw a knife-throwing exhibition and was intrigued. I bought my daggers and started practicin'. That was about the same time as I learned to use a six-gun and a saddle gun. I'm not sure if you've noticed before but Lady Justice has the Scales of Justice in one hand and a sword in the other hand."

The marshal thought for a moment and then nodded. "Are you as proficient with your guns as you seem to be with your knives?"

"I guess I'm somewhat proficient when I need to be."

"John, I'm sure that's an understatement," said the marshal. "I guess I can also understand why you feel carrying a badge would be a burden to you."

"Thanks for understandin', Marshal. What I can tell you is I'll keep you informed as I'm trackin' Granger."

"I 'preciate that."

"One more thing I need, Marshal. I've got a good description of Granger but I don't have any idea about the looks of the other men. Could you describe 'em for me?"

"I'm glad to, John. Let's start with Quentin. He is about five foot, ten. He always wears a new black hat. He must go through several hats each year to make sure they always look new. Quentin also always wears a black shirt and a bright yellow bandana around his neck. I don't remember much more about him. Oh yes, he wears his gun low and carries a big knife on his belt. It's at an angle so he can reach across and draw it with his right hand.

"Now Skyler and Morgan—well, they're always together. If you find one of 'em, you'll find the other not too far away. Skyler is more the leader of the two. If there's a town nearby, you can always find both brothers in a saloon from the middle of the afternoon on. They like to drink and play cards and look for fights. It's easy to tell they're brothers 'cause they look a lot alike. Both have light blond hair. The last time I saw 'em, their hair was long and hung down their backs in ponytails. I don't recall much more about 'em. They're about the same height as Quentin.

"Oh yes, Quentin rides a paint and Skyler and Morgan both ride palominos. Beautiful horses, all three."

"Thanks, Marshal. That helps a lot. I'll be headed out in the mornin' for Austin. You probably have a better chance of findin' Granger goin' north. But I just can't shake the feelin' that he could be goin' back to some of the places he's been before. He may even have other loot he's buried he wants to dig up."

"He might at that. John, I'm glad I met you. And I sure wish you lived in Fredericksburg 'cause I could use you as a deputy. But to be fair, you would be a better marshal and I could be your deputy."

"I 'preciate the compliment, Marshal. But I've seen how you have the respect of the citizens here. Fredericksburg has a good man as their marshal."

"That means a lot, John."

"Marshal, I do have a question. Not meaning to criticize but it looks like your courthouse has seen its better day. Does it provide adequately for the community?"

"Funny you should ask 'cause several of us have been tryin' to get interest in buildin' a new one. The problem is we just don't have the money it'll take. We did have a committee study it last year. We're the seat of Gillespie County. As they looked at the projected growth of the county and the size of courthouse that's needed, they estimated it would cost nearly fifty thousand dollars to build. That was the end of the study committee. They knew we didn't have the money and didn't have a way to raise it. So as inadequate as it is, we'll just have to live with it."

"Marshal, I know some people in New York who may be willin' to help with that. When I get to Austin, I'm gonna send 'em a telegram and see if they have an interest in helping."

"That would be great, John. But I can't imagine why anyone in New York would want to help a town in Texas."

"I don't know. I've heard they've helped with some other things that seemed just about as unlikely."

John and Wilson shook hands and John went over to the livery stable to groom Midnight. After caring for his horse and paying for some oats, John went to the hotel and got a room for the night.

"Is there some place around here where I can get somethin' to eat," John asked the hotel clerk. "I've been to Fraulein Hilda's and it's fine food but I was thinkin' I'd like something other than German cookin' tonight."

"There's a Pretty Good Wife," said the clerk.

"Who's that?"

"It's not a who but a what," said the clerk. "The café down the street is called A Pretty Good Wife. Some just call it the Wife, like, 'I'm gonna be eatin' at the Wife.' Others call it Pretty, like 'I just had breakfast at Pretty's.'"

John thanked the clerk and headed down to the Pretty Good Wife. The café was crowded even though it was late. Crudder ordered a steak, a baked potato, and a slice of apple pie. It was a good meal but throughout the meal he continued to have flashbacks of the awful scene at Stonewall. He had a feeling he would be haunted by memories of what he had seen for a long time.

CHAPTER 12

John woke up early, had breakfast back at Pretty's and then saddled Midnight. As he came out of the livery, he saw Marshal Wilson arriving at his office. He waved and the marshal returned the gesture as he trotted down the road to head to Austin. As soon as he was clear of the last buildings, he leaned forward in the saddle and Midnight went instantly into a gallop. After a few minutes he settled back into a lope.

About an hour later, John slowed Midnight to a trot. He knew just ahead was Stonewall. He hated to pass the gruesome scene again. As he passed the corral, he noticed the carcasses had bloated and had drawn significantly more flies than the day before. He didn't envy the men whose job it was to bury the large animals. Theirs was a backbreaking job that would turn the stomachs of the strongest men.

Leaving Stonewall, John got Midnight to trot. It was obvious Midnight wanted to go faster but John knew they wouldn't make Austin until the middle of the next day. There was no use in hurrying and tiring Midnight needlessly. John needed the saddle time to try to make sense of what he had witnessed. He also knew he needed to get on the trail of Granger's gang.

By evening, John was looking for a campsite when he saw evidence of a town ahead. He saw a sign that said Dripping Springs, Texas. John smiled to himself at the name and at the possibility for him to get a hot meal and a bed.

He went to the marshal's office but found the office empty. John looked down the street and saw only four businesses: a saloon with a hotel next door, a café, and a livery stable. The town looked like all it lacked was a church, a general store, and a blacksmith.

Crudder led Midnight to the saloon. Sure enough he found the marshal inside. He introduced himself and bought the marshal a beer.

"Glad to meet you, Mr. Crudder," said the marshal. "I'm Pete Akins. Everybody just calls me Pete. So, you used to be a marshal, you say. Where'd you serve?"

"I was in Bandera and I still live there, but Clem Williams is the marshal there now. And just call me John."

"What can I do for you, John?"

"Well, Marshal, I'm looking for some men. A man named Granger and three other men. Have you seen 'em?"

"I'll say I have. They were here just a few minutes ago. They were playin' poker with some of the men. Directly a fight broke out. I was able to break it up before anyone got shot."

"Where'd they go?" asked John.

"The other men said they were cheatin'. I don't doubt it. I told 'em they had a choice. They could all go to jail or they could clear out. They said they were stayin' at the hotel but I told them the only place they could sleep in town tonight was in the jail. They didn't like that much. Granger said I was gonna regret treatin' him that way. But I ain't afraid of him. I told him they could find a good place to camp out at Onion Creek just out of town. They bought several bottles of whisky and left. They haven't been gone more than thirty minutes."

"Marshal, you're lucky to still be alive. I've just come from Fredericksburg. Granger and his gang murdered nine people at the stage stop at Stonewall. One was a baby." Crudder stood abruptly. "Good bye, Marshal. I'm goin' after 'em."

The marshal's face paled as he realized how close he had come to getting into a fight with the outlaw gang. "Hold on young feller, you ain't the law around here. If there's any 'goin' after' to be done, I'll do it."

"Marshal, you don't know who you're dealin' with. A few days ago, Granger tortured and killed an elderly couple in Bandera. He blew up their house with the woman inside. In Stonewall, the gang blew up the stagecoach with all the passengers inside. They killed the driver and the guard. It also looks like before the stage arrived, they ate breakfast at the stage stop and then paid their bill with lead. The old couple who ran the stop were both slaughtered."

The marshal's jaw was slack as he contemplated what he was hearing. "Crudder, it don't sound like either one of us can handle that bunch. What we need is a posse."

"That's fine with me, Marshal. But you need to know I'm goin' after 'em tonight. If you want to get a posse together, get it done and let's quit wastin' time."

The marshal got up and yelled, "You men listen to me. I need your help and I need it now." The saloon got quiet and the marshal continued. "You know Granger and the bunch that was with him? The men who were cheatin' you at cards?" Several nodded and voiced their acknowledgment. "This young man just came from Stonewall. He said they murdered nine people. One of them was a baby. They've also murdered people in Bandera just a few days ago."

"They're also wanted in Austin, San Anton, and Kerrville for murder and bank robbery," John added.

"So, men, I sent 'em out to camp by Onion Creek. We can't take a chance on 'em gettin' away. I want a posse to come with me right now. Who'll ride with us?"

Ten men stepped forward to be sworn in. "Now men, listen up. We've got to be quiet if we are gonna get the drop on them. I figure we'll walk our horses out 'til we get near Onion Creek. We'll split up and come at 'em from both sides. But be careful and don't shoot each other. The four we're after will be right around their campfire.

"We'll walk the last half mile so we can slip up on 'em. Don't nobody shoot until I give the signal. I'll take the first shot and will call out to 'em and say they're surrounded and they need to give up. Watch 'em close, if they go for their guns, take 'em all out.

"John Crudder here used to be the marshal in Bandera. Anything you want to add, John?"

"I agree with the marshal about bein' careful you don't shoot each other. One thing I would suggest, is that you use a saddle gun, if you've got one, and shoot from behind a tree. I don't think this bunch will give up so when you hear the marshal's shot, take a bead on the man nearest you. Get ready to fire if they make a move for their guns."

"Thank you, John. Now you men raise your right hand so I can swear you in." The men raised their hands and waited for the marshal. "Do you swear to uphold the law? Say, 'I swear.'"

"I swear," came the thunderous response. Crudder declined to raise his hand but no one noticed.

"Let's go, men," said Marshal Atkins. "It's dark out there so we're not gonna get in a hurry. When we get near the creek, I'll take half of you men with me and the other half can go with Crudder." The marshal assigned each man to a group and then went outside and got on his horse.

It took about fifteen minutes to get to the place where they tied their horses. John took his group and went around to the left. The marshal went to the right. John was impressed that the men were quiet and calm.

Silently, they crept through brush. There was a half-moon so they were able to avoid hazards. None of the men were in a hurry. John hoped since the gang had bought several bottles of whisky, they would be drunk and passed out when the posse arrived.

John could see the flicker of their campfire ahead. He held up his hand and all the men stopped instantly. He pointed to the campfire to make sure the men had seen it. They nodded in response. John pointed to each man and then to a location around the fire. The men split up and took their positions around the camp.

With each man in place, they waited for the signal to come from the marshal. They waited for ten minutes for the marshal's group to get in place. Finally, the signal came. There was a single rifle shot into the air.

"You men in camp. This is Marshal Atkins. You're surrounded and you're under arrest. Raise your hands now!"

All four men rolled away from the fire and came up with their guns blazing. The posse shot but none of the bullets found their mark. Gunfire continued to be exchanged as John crept from tree to tree to get closer to the fire.

A man to John's left let out a groan when he was hit. He fell to the ground and didn't move again. At the same time, John heard several horses gallop off but he knew there were still outlaws in the camp returning the fire of the posse.

Someone yelled, "They shot the marshal. Let's get 'em men." There was a hail of bullets but most of them went wide and far from their mark. John had yet to fire. He knew it was pointless unless he had a target. The men had moved around so much that it was difficult to discriminate the posse from the gang members. In the flicker of the fire, John made out a long ponytail hanging from one man's head. It was light-colored so John felt sure he was looking at either Skyler or Morgan. He took aim and shot the man in the head.

"Skyler!" came a shout from someone nearby. The man who shouted moved over to his fallen comrade and John was able to make out that he too had a long ponytail. He lined up his second target and shot that man in the head.

"This is John Crudder. Posse, quit shooting. Two of the gang are dead and I think two have gotten away. Stand easy and keep watch. I'm gonna check to make sure there's no more threat."

Crudder slipped up to the fire and clearly saw the bodies of the two men. He kicked the guns from their hands. "All clear," shouted John. "Our horses are too far away for us to give chase. See if you can find the horses for these two men. At least two of us can give chase."

"All of their horses are gone," came a shout from the other side of the campfire. "The two that got away must have shooed away the other horses. What a heartless thing to do to their compadres."

"Somebody check on the marshal," shouted John. "And see if anyone else got shot."

"The marshal's dead," came a reply.

From behind John came another voice. "And they got Jacobs."

"Is anyone else hurt?" asked John. The murmured response let him know the other men were fine. "Let's go get our horses. We need to get these bodies back to town. Is there a telegraph office in town?"

"Yes, sir," came a response. "It's right behind the marshal's office and the telegraph operator sleeps in the office."

"You men take care of the marshal and the other bodies," said John. "I'm headed back to town to send out some messages."

Crudder went back to where the horses were tied, mounted Midnight and let him trot back to town. He found the telegraph office with the operator sitting at his desk reading.

"I need to send out some messages," said John.

"Yes, sir," replied the operator. "Just write them out and I'll send them directly."

John got paper and pen from the desk and sat down close to the lamp and began to write. He knew Wilson was out on posse but he hoped someone would be able to track his whereabouts.

Deputy Marshal Buford
Fredericksburg, Texas

Try to track down Marshal Wilson in Llano, Mason, and Marble Falls. Found gang in Dripping Springs. Granger and Quentin escaped. Skyler and Morgan dead. Marshal Atkins dead. Headed to Austin.

John Crudder
Dripping Springs, Texas

He took another piece of paper to write home.

Slim Hanson
Bandera, Texas

Two of gang dead. Granger and one other on the run. I'm headed to Austin in the morning. Give my love to Charlotte and the girls.

John Crudder
Dripping Springs, Texas

There was one final telegram to send.

Howard Hastings
Fifth Avenue, New York City

Send $50,000 for new courthouse in Fredericksburg in care of Marshal Wilson. Please give update on Alvelda, addressed to Bandera.

John Crudder
Dripping Springs, Texas

John stood by as the operator sent the messages and then laid three silver dollars on the desk and went outside in time to see the posse return with the four dead bodies. They hitched their horses where the posse had started, in front of the saloon. The men carefully took the bodies of the marshal and Jacobs and laid them on the boardwalk. Then they unceremoniously dumped the two dead outlaws in the street.

"If you'll tell me where the undertaker is," said John, "I'll go make arrangements."

"We don't have an undertaker," replied one of the men. "But we do have some coffins ready to go, behind the livery stable. Men, let's take the bodies over there."

The men reverently picked up the bodies of their own and carried them to the livery and gently laid each in a coffin. Two other men dragged the corpses of the outlaws and plopped their bodies in coffins and nailed the lids in place.

John hoped the café was still open. He walked across the street and found it was. While he didn't have much appetite, he knew he needed to eat something in order to have the strength needed to stop the rest of the gang.

After he ate, he took Midnight to the livery and gave him a good brushing. He spoke softly to the great steed telling him what a good job he had done. Midnight whinnied and dipped his head in response. John got him a bucket of oats knowing he would settle up with the proprietor in the morning.

John took a room at the hotel. As he drifted off to sleep, he wondered what the new day would bring.

CHAPTER 13

The Road to Driftwood, Texas

Granger and Quentin ran to their horses as bullets were flying all around them. As they mounted up, Granger grabbed the reins of the palomino mares Skyler and Morgan rode and pulled them behind his horse. They broke into a gallop and rode hard to the south.

To his surprise, they found a road and were able to continue at a full gallop thanks to the moonlight. After half an hour of hard riding, Granger let go of the two riderless horses and slowed his own horse to a walk.

"Why'd you take their horses?" asked Quentin.

"'Cause I didn't want any of the posse usin' 'em to come after us. And I also didn't want Skyler and Morgan comin' with us. With them not havin' horses to ride, they had to stay and fight, lettin' us get away. Besides, there'll be more loot for us."

Quentin thought Granger was the nastiest man he had ever met.

He didn't dare voice his beliefs for he knew it would only put Granger into a murderous rage.

"The brothers had started gettin' on my nerves," said Granger. "It was a mistake makin' brothers part of the gang. They always stuck together and had too much influence on what we did. Anyway, with us on the run, it'll be a lot easier to get away with it just bein' two of us. Four riders together attract too much attention."

Quentin knew Granger was right. "That makes sense, boss. That was a good decision." Quentin knew Granger was as dangerous as a stick of dynamite lying by a campfire.

"I'm not sure what's ahead of us but there has to be a town before long. Let's speed up and see if we can make it before mornin'. I wouldn't put it past the posse to be on our trail right now."

The horses maintained a trot for another half an hour and came to a sign.

Driftwood, Texas
Population 122

The only light they could see was coming from the saloon. Granger and Quentin tied their horses to the hitching rail and went inside and ordered a bottle of whisky. There were several people drinking and playing cards. No one seemed to have any interest in the two strangers. That was just fine with Granger.

He took the bottle to a table and poured each a glass of the amber liquid. "I guess we showed ol' Atkins. When he ran us out of town, I knew he was as good as dead. I'd have ridden back in the mornin' and shot him."

"I wonder why he chased us out and then brought a posse after us?" asked Quentin. "It would have been smarter to have arrested us in the saloon."

"That's because he didn't have any cause to arrest us in the saloon. He hadn't seen any posters on us so he didn't know we was wanted."

"So, why'd he decide to come after us?" asked Quentin.

"Somebody must've come to town after we left and told the marshal about us. It was probably somebody who knew about Stonewall. Quentin, I think that means we've got someone chasin' us. I shor thought the posse would've thought we went north from Stonewall."

"I wonder who's after us?" asked Quentin.

"How am I supposed to know? It could be anybody."

They drained their glasses and Granger poured another round. The men drank in silence as they considered who might be chasing them. After another round, they walked next door to the hotel and got rooms for the night.

* * *

Granger and Quentin slept until middle of the morning. When they woke up, they went to the café for breakfast.

"What can I get you gentlemen?" asked the young waitress.

"Well, we can start with you," said Granger. "Aren't you a sweet thing."

He reached around her waist and pulled her down into his lap and laughed at the surprised look on her face.

"That'll be enough," said a voice from the kitchen. A man emerged carrying a shotgun. "You can let her go right now."

"I don't think so, friend," said Granger. "I think this sweet thing is gonna join us for breakfast. Ain't that right, sweet thing?"

The man raised the shotgun and said, "I said let her go."

"Sure thing, mister," said Granger. "I'll let her go." As the woman got off his lap, Granger pulled his six-gun and shot the man twice in the chest. The woman screamed.

"You've killed my husband!" She cried as she ran to where the dead man had fallen and cradled his head in her lap. "Why'd you kill him? He didn't do nothing to you."

"He was about to shoot me with that shotgun. Everybody here saw it. Didn't you?" Granger turned to the stunned people at the table next to him. "You saw him threaten me, didn't you?"

The man and woman at the table couldn't utter a sound but nodded their heads in agreement. Then he turned to another table where three men were eating. "You saw him threaten me, didn't you?" The men nodded in agreement. Granger got up and went to each table and exacted the same agreement that he was in the right.

The door to the café opened and the marshal came in with his gun out but not pointed at anyone in particular. "What's goin' on here?"

"Well, Marshal," said Granger. "I'm glad you're here but I wish you had gotten here earlier. This man threatened to shoot me with that scatter gun. I didn't have no choice but to defend myself. Everybody saw it. Ain't that right?"

Granger turned to several tables and saw all heads nodding in agreement. "See there, Marshal. It's just as I said. I didn't have no choice."

"That's a lie!" shouted the distraught waitress. "He pulled me onto his lap and my husband told him to let me go."

"Now, hon, you know you were enjoyin' sittin' in my lap. I didn't do nothin' to hurt you. Everybody here will back me on that."

"You're an evil man," she shouted. "You killed him for nothing. He was defending me."

"I'm real sorry about your husband, miss. But he didn't give me no choice."

"Stop saying that. You killed him and you enjoyed it!"

"All right, you men," said the marshal motioning to Granger and Quentin. "It's time for you to get out of town. And we don't want you back here again."

"But we haven't had our breakfast yet," said Granger. "This lady hadn't even gotten us any coffee."

"I said it's time for you to ride out," said the marshal. "You men saddle up and get."

"All right, Marshal," said Granger. "But you need to know I don't take kindly to people talkin' to me the way you are."

The marshal leveled his gun at Granger and said, "I said ride out—now!"

Granger and Quentin got up and headed for the door. "We're goin', Marshal. You're not bein' very hospitable. That's all I can say." Quentin walked out the door as Granger turned a bit to hide his gun hand. He turned quickly and shot the marshal before he knew what was happening. The marshal was dead before he hit the ground.

"Now, does anyone else have anything they want to say to me?" asked Granger. "How about you, sweet thing. You were real mouthy a while ago. Do you have anythin' you want to say to me?"

The waitress's grief had given way to shock as she saw the marshal murdered. She shook her head and said nothing.

"Anybody else got anything to say?"

The patrons shook their heads and said nothing. Granger saw a bit of movement from a man who had his hands beneath the table. Granger swung his gun around and shot him in the head.

"Now that weren't real smart," said Granger. "Anybody else want to go for their gun?" All the patrons made sure their hands were on top of their tables. "Anyone else want to try me?" The men present shook their heads.

"Quentin, go to the kitchen and get us somethin' to eat." Then he turned to address the stunned patrons. "Now we're gettin' ready to leave. If you don't value your lives then you can mount up and come after us. We'll leave you just as dead as these three men. In fact, I hope you come after us. I'd enjoy watching the life drain from your faces."

Quentin brought out some biscuits and sausage. He and Granger put the sausage between the biscuits and devoured several while they stood in the café. They were in no hurry to leave. "Sweet thing, we need some coffee. And I want it right now!"

The trembling waitress quickly got up, poured two cups full and brought them to the table where Granger and Quentin were standing. Both men sat down. "Look what you're doin'," yelled Granger. "You're spillin' coffee all over the place."

"I'm sorry, mister. Please don't hurt me. I'll get you some more."

Granger let out a loud belly laugh. "That's all right, sweet thing. You don't have to get us more. But I do like the way you're talking to me now. You know, I may come back in a few days to see if you'd like to spend some quiet time with me."

The poor young woman had a terrified look on her face and immediately put both hands to her mouth. Granger cackled an evil laugh. "Don't worry, sweet thing. I think you'd like me when you got to know me. Come on, Quentin, let's get goin'. And sweet thing, you think about me while I'm gone. I'll be lookin' forward to seein' you again soon.

"And you men, you better think twice before you decide to ride after us. I've killed so many people that a few more won't matter at all to me."

Granger and Quentin walked out of the café and surveyed the street. No one was stirring. Evidently everyone had taken cover and they weren't willing to challenge the strangers. Granger pulled his gun and looked up and down the street to see if there was anyone laying in wait for him. Satisfied no one would follow, they mounted up and rode out of town.

As their horses disappeared down the road, the citizens slowly came out of their hiding places. The café customers emerged from the room that contained three dead bodies. Some of the men dragged the dead men out to the boardwalk. A crowd gathered around and spoke softly to one another.

"Isn't anyone gonna go after them?" shouted the distraught waitress.

The men looked at each other and slowly shook their heads.

"Are you all cowards?" she asked. "You're just going to let them come into our town and commit murder and get away scot-free?" The men just hung their heads in shame. The new widow sunk to the ground crying and pulled her dead husband's head into her lap. She rocked forward and backward as though she were caring for an infant.

CHAPTER 14

Austin, Texas

John rode into Austin hoping he would run into Granger and Quentin. Little did he know they had turned south and gone to Driftwood. Crudder rode down Congress Avenue past the capital and stopped at the Texas Rangers office.

Inside, he inquired as to who was in charge and was told that would be Captain Jessup. Jessup came out of the office at the back of the room and introduced himself to Crudder.

"Pleased to meet you, Captain. I'm John Crudder. I used to be the marshal in Bandera. Do you have a few minutes I could visit with you?"

"Sure, Mr. Crudder. Come on back."

"Thank you, Captain. Just call me John."

John followed him back to his office noting there had not been an offer to call the captain by his first name.

"Now, what can I do for you, John?"

"Well, sir, I know Marshal Williams from Bandera contacted you about Butch Granger and his gang. I've got some new information you may not have yet."

"I'd like to hear it, John. What can you tell me about Granger?"

"Well, I guess it was about three days ago, Granger and his gang rode into the stagecoach station at Stonewall. They murdered the couple who ran the general store and stage stop. Then when the stage arrived, they blew up the stage with all of the passengers inside."

The captain's face registered the shock he was feeling. "What? Who could be so cruel?"

"Captain, there were three women and a man in the coach. There was also a little baby. Their bodies were destroyed by the blast. They also murdered the driver and guard. We found the strongbox empty but there was flour all around. It looked to us like they used flour sacks to hold the gold. But there was so much of it they couldn't carry it far. We followed the traces of flour and found where they buried the gold. I'm pretty sure what we recovered was the full contents of what was stolen 'cause we took the gold from the flour sacks and put it back in the strongbox and it was completely full."

"Well, I'm glad you recovered the gold. You kept sayin' 'we.' Who else was with you?"

"After I discovered the bodies in Stonewall, I rode back into Fredericksburg and got Marshal Wilson and his deputy, Buford, to come and investigate the crime scene. After the marshal investigated, we started searchin' for the gold, thinkin' they couldn't have gone far with it. We found it a few hundred yards off the road."

"I know Marshal Wilson. He's a fine man," said the captain.

"I couldn't agree more," said Crudder. "He's a dedicated lawman. And his deputy is also doin' a fine job."

"Thank you, John. I'll make sure we get word out to the Rangers who are in the field so they can be on the lookout for the gang. Is there anything else to report?"

"Well, Granger slaughtered the horses in Stonewall. He killed all four of the stage horses while they were still in harness. Then he went to the corral and killed all the relief horses. There were twelve horses in all."

"That's consistent with what we know about Granger. He loves killin' animals as much as he does people. Only someone with a very disturbed mind would be so mean."

"You're right about that, Captain. I wish that was all I had to report but there's more."

"Go ahead, John. What else is there?"

"Well, Marshal Wilson got a posse and headed north out of Fredericksburg. We both thought it made sense that Granger would head away from places where he was wanted for his crimes. But I thought it would be good to head here just to see if he came back to Austin."

"I don't think he's in Austin," said the captain. "If he is, he's keeping a lot lower profile than he ever has before."

"I agree he's probably not in Austin after all. However, last night, I rode into Dripping Springs and found out Granger and his gang had just gotten thrown out of the saloon for cheatin' only thirty minutes before. I told Marshal Atkins about the slaughter at Stonewall and he got together a posse and we tracked Granger to their campin' place just out of town.

"We surprised the gang and killed two of them; Skyler and Morgan. Unfortunately Marshal Atkins and a man named Jacobs also got killed. Granger and Quentin escaped. I'm not sure where they went. Our horses were tied far down the road. Granger even took off with the other two horses so Skyler and Morgan wouldn't have had any chance of escapin'. Granger was sacrificing his own men so he could escape."

The captain listened and nodded as John recounted the story. Occasionally, the captain would pause and write down some of the details John was giving. John hoped getting word out to the rest of the Rangers would result in Granger and Quentin being captured— or killed. He knew they had to be found soon before they killed others.

"John, thanks for ridin' in here and givin' me this report. I'll be gettin' word out to the Rangers who are coverin' this part of Texas. We'll catch him. You can depend on it. What are your plans now?"

"Well, Captain, I'm not sure. If I knew where Granger was, I'd chase after him but I don't have any idea where he is now. I just wanted to ride here and let you know of his latest crimes."

"Now John, I realize you used to be a lawman but you're not one any more. Leave the chasin' of Granger to me and the boys."

"I'll take that under consideration, captain. What I can promise you is I'll not get in your way or compromise any law enforcement efforts. But I can also promise you that the Jackson's in Bandera were friends of mine. I won't rest 'til Granger and Quentin are brought to justice. And Captain, I'll never be able to forget the mangled body of the baby and the other stage passengers in Stonewall. These men need to be brought to justice."

"Well, I can't blame you for that, John. Raise your hand and let me swear you in. I can tell you're a good investigator. We can use another good Ranger."

"Thanks, Captain. But if it's all the same to you, I'd rather not. I know you would need to be able to direct me to investigate other crimes. I'm not willin' to take on the burden of carrying a badge again."

"Suit yourself, John. But I wish you'd reconsider."

"I take that as a compliment, Captain. Well, I better be gettin' on."

John stood and extended his hand to the captain. They shook hands and John went out to the hitching rail and mounted Midnight. He went down the street to Stinky Shirley's Saloon. John recalled the last time he was here—he had been to the State Police office. The Rangers had been dissolved after the end of the war and replaced by a police force that was thought to be less inclined to continue to think of themselves as Confederates. But with the end of reconstruction came the reinstatement of the Texas Rangers.

John was pleased to find Stinky Shirley's also served food. He ordered a steak and a cup of coffee and contemplated his next move. John also wondered where the saloon got its name, just as he had when he was here before. But once again, he declined to ask about its origin preferring instead to fill in the blanks with his imagination. He smiled to himself as he considered the possibilities. Then as he recalled the carnage left behind by Granger and the gang, he gritted his teeth as he considered the lopsided Scales of Justice. He made a silent vow to make sure the remaining gang members were brought to justice soon.

CHAPTER 15

Captain Jessup immediately sent out telegrams to the Texas Rangers who were on patrol in the area. All the telegrams were the same and simply addressed to "Texas Ranger." The custom of the Rangers was to immediately check in at the telegraph office when entering a town to see if there were any messages and to let the telegraph operator know where to find them if a message came in.

Texas Ranger

Highest Priority. Butch Granger and gang murdered nine in Stonewall. Blew up stage with all passengers still aboard, including a baby. Also killed twelve horses. Last seen in Dripping Springs last night. Murdered Marshal Atkins and another man. Two members of gang dead. Granger and Quentin still at large. Use caution. Report sightings immediately.

Captain Jessup
Texas Rangers, Austin, Texas

Fifteen Rangers in the Hill Country and Central Texas received the telegram. Immediately other cases they were working on became lesser priorities. Within hours of transmitting the message, most of the telegrams had been read by Rangers. One of the telegrams was sent to San Saba, a community of about three hundred due north of Fredericksburg, named for the San Saba River, which runs through the town.

Fredericksburg's Marshal Wilson was riding alone. The rest of the posse had gone back home to take care of personal business. While he was angry at the men for deserting their mission, he knew it was unreasonable for him to expect the men to give up their responsibilities at home for an extended period. He also realized he would soon need to follow suit for he had to get back to his marshaling duties. As he rode into town, he went to the telegraph office to send a message to his deputy.

The telegraph operator saw his badge. "Hey mister. Are you a Ranger?"

"No, I'm Marshal Wilson from Fredericksburg. Why do you ask?"

"'Cause I just received this telegram that was addressed to 'Texas Ranger.' I guess with you being a lawman and all, you should read it."

Wilson read the message and immediately changed his plans. He took a pen and paper from the desk and wrote a different message to his deputy.

Deputy Marshal Buford
Fredericksburg, Texas

Granger seen in Dripping Springs last night. Murdered
Marshal Atkins and another man. I'm going there now.

Marshal Wilson
San Saba, Texas

Wilson thanked the operator and laid a silver dollar on the desk. He mounted his horse and headed south. The marshal estimated it would take him about three days to make it to Dripping Springs. He knew by that time, Granger would be long gone. Lacking a better plan, Wilson decided he would stop at every town he passed and check in with the local marshal to see if there was any sign of Granger and his gang. He knew Granger was unpredictable. Just maybe he would cross trails with the outlaw and be able to bring him to justice.

At midday, Wilson passed through Cherokee, named for Cherokee Creek, which ran nearby. Having just come this way the day before, he knew Granger had not been there and could not have traveled there from Dripping Springs in a single day.

After a day of hard riding, Wilson made it to Llano for the night. He stabled his horse for the evening and took a room at the boarding house. After supper, he took out his map and plotted the rest of his journey.

The next morning, Wilson followed the Llano River south. He slowed his pace a bit knowing speed was not as big of a factor as was keenly observing his surroundings. Wilson was aware Granger would not think twice about bushwhacking a passing traveler.

By evening, Wilson arrived in Kingsland. Kingsland was named for Martin King, who, along with J.M. Tussell, established the town where the Llano and Colorado Rivers met. Wilson went to the marshal's office but found the marshal had already left. He left his horse tied and walked down the street to the café.

Entering the café, he spotted a man with a badge and introduced himself.

"Howdy, Marshal. I'm Marshal Junior Wilson from Fredericksburg."

"Have a seat, Marshal. I'm Marshal William Yates. But everyone calls me Bill." He extended his hand to Wilson. They shook and Wilson sat down.

"What brings you to Kingsland, Junior?"

Wilson ordered a steak and hung his hat on the back of his chair. "I'm after Butch Granger. They call him 'The Butcher.' Ever heard of him?"

"Can't say as I have. What's he wanted for?"

"Granger and his gang are wanted for several murders, bank robbery, and other crimes. But I'm after him for murdering nine people at a stage stop just outside of my town. He put dynamite inside a stagecoach filled with passengers, killing all of 'em including a little baby."

Yates stopped eating and stared at Wilson. "I've never heard of anything so brutal."

"Seems like what Granger likes best," said Wilson, "is usin' dynamite on people and shootin' animals. He's blown up other people and typically kills all livestock as well as dogs and cats he encounters. When he blew up the stage, he also killed a dozen horses."

"Where do you think Granger is now?" asked Yates.

"Not really sure. Two nights ago, he was in Dripping Springs. He killed Marshal Atkins and another man. Wherever he is, you can bet he's up to no good. Probably killed someone else. My guess is he'll not stop his killin' 'til he's locked up or shot dead."

"How can I help, Junior?"

"Just be on the alert," said Wilson. "I wanted you to know about Granger in case he heads this way. Some of his gang have been killed but there's a man named Quentin that's still ridin' with him. Quentin is 'bout as bad as Granger."

"I'll shor keep an eye out for 'em." Yates continued eating and contemplating what he had learned from Wilson. "Where you headed next, Junior?"

"I'm not certain. My plan is to keep headin' south and east and see if there have been any sign of Granger in any towns I come to."

Yates thought for a moment. "About twenty to twenty-five miles, you'll come to Smithwick Mills. It is due southeast of here."

"I guess that's where I'm headed." Wilson continued eating his supper. When he was finished, he shook hands with Marshal Yates again, collected his horse from the marshal's office, took her to the livery stable, and got a room at the hotel just across the street. Wilson had a feeling he was going to cross paths with Granger before he returned to Fredericksburg.

CHAPTER 16

Bee Caves, Texas

Granger and Quentin knew there were many people looking for them. They moved north to Bee Caves, just west of Austin. The town got its name from caves that swarmed with Mexican honeybees on the banks of Barton Creek.

They slipped into town in the evening and wanted to be able to lay low for several days. To accomplish this, they determined they would not do any drinking in the saloon but would buy their whisky and take it back to their rooms at the hotel. And since they weren't going to be hanging out at the saloon, they wouldn't be playing any poker—another activity that often led them into trouble.

Granger confined his travel about town to the hotel and the livery stable. Quentin, less well known, was designated the purchaser of liquor from the saloon, tending the horses at the livery stable, and getting supplies at the general store. They were able to blend in with the citizens of Bee Caves—especially since Granger never came out of his room.

Their plan worked well for about three days until Granger felt his room getting smaller and smaller. He occupied his time playing solitaire, drinking whisky, and eating meals Quentin brought him from the café. But he had to get out, even if it meant they had to move on to another town.

That evening, Granger and Quentin went to the saloon to spend the evening drinking and playing cards. As far as Granger could tell, no one recognized him and no one acted suspicious of the two newcomers. The saloon was busy so they had no trouble finding people willing to take them on in a poker game.

As the evening passed, Granger and Quentin won more games than they lost. They were careful to let the local rubes win some. But Granger grew impatient. He knew he could beat anyone at cards so he started winning every hand. Soon others had gathered around the table to watch the stranger who had all the luck.

On one hand, Granger slickly pulled an ace out of his sleeve, discarded another card, and placed the winning hand on the table.

"Hey, he's cheatin'!" yelled a man standing behind Granger.

Granger pushed away from the table, wheeled around, and shot the man before he had any chance to defend himself.

"Does anybody else think I'm cheatin'?"

✳ ✳ ✳

Marshal Wilson made it to Smithwick Mills but didn't find any sign of Granger. He spent the night at the hotel in town and headed out the next morning for Bee Caves. After a day of traveling, he camped just off the road and built a fire to make some coffee and to heat up a can of beans.

That evening, Wilson couldn't shake the feeling he was closing in on Granger. After supper he tried to sleep but realized he lay awake most of the night. He finally got to sleep somewhere before dawn and then slept soundly until the middle of the morning. Wilson awoke to the sun in his face.

He hurriedly rekindled his fire, heated up some coffee, and cooked a chunk of bacon he speared with a stick. Wilson put out his campfire and mounted his mare for the ride to Bee Caves. The day was hot already and got hotter as he rode. His horse was showing the wear of hard riding over several days. He took the journey a bit slower and stopped at every stream to rest his horse and drink some water.

It was well after dark when he arrived at Bee Caves. He knew there was little chance of finding Granger this time of the evening. All Wilson could think about was getting a good meal and having a bed to sleep in for the evening.

He spotted the café and rode his horse up to the hitching rail and swung down. As he was tying his horse, he looked over at the saloon next door. There was plenty of noise coming from inside. Much of what he heard was laughing but he also heard some loud moans. He guessed a poker game was well underway.

There were several horses tied to the hitching rails in front of the saloons. As was his habit, he quickly surveyed the mounts.

When he spotted a paint in the group, his pulse quickened. He recalled hearing Quentin rode a paint. While he couldn't recall anyone ever saying what Granger rode, he felt the need to check out the other horses. Two horses down from the paint, he found a horse whose saddle had the initials *BG* carved into the back jockey. He walked around to the other side and on the back jockey found the word *Butch* carefully tooled into the saddle.

There was no doubt he was getting ready to come face-to-face with Granger and Quentin. He pulled his six-gun and carefully made his way to the outer wall of the saloon. The chatter inside was becoming louder. He carefully peeked over the swinging door to see if he could find Granger.

The room was filled with smoke. Toward the back of the room he saw a table that was surrounded by spectators apparently watching a poker game. Wilson tried to get a look at who was at the table but couldn't see anyone who was sitting because of the onlookers. One man stepped aside for a moment allowing the marshal to get a quick glance at the table.

Wilson saw only one man. He was wearing an immaculate black hat, a black shirt, and had a bright yellow bandana tied around his neck. The man he was staring at was Quentin. There was no mistaking it.

The marshal backed out of the doorway and tried to come up with a plan as to how to close in on Granger and Quentin so he could arrest them without getting anyone else hurt. Briefly he considered coming in the back door. He also thought about walking to the bar, getting a beer, and then moseying to the back of the room to get behind Granger.

"Hey, he's cheatin'!" yelled a man standing behind Granger.

Granger pushed away from the table, wheeled around, and shot the man before he had any chance to defend himself. The crowd watching the poker game as well as the other men at the table instantly melted away, leaving only Granger and Quentin.

"Does anybody else think I'm cheatin'?"

"I do," shouted Wilson as he walked into the saloon with his gun leveled at Granger.

Granger and Quentin upturned the table and got behind it as Wilson fired his gun. Immediately, Granger and Quentin opened fire on Wilson, dropping him on the floor.

"Now let's play some more poker," said Granger. Quentin righted the table and picked up the money that was in the pot. "Who wants to try their luck against me and Quentin?"

People continued moving away from Granger. Several stepped over Wilson's body and slipped out the door. "Doesn't anyone want to try to beat me?" Granger shouted with a sneer on his face. "I promise to let you win—some of the time."

Quentin laughed at the joke and Granger joined in. "Don't let the dead bodies bother you. We can move 'em out of the way and keep playin'." Both men laughed much harder at Granger's taunt.

"Well, if you're not gonna sit down so I can win the money fair and square, then I'm just gonna have to ask each of you to empty your pockets and put all your money on this table. Don't anyone try to leave without paying up. Now come on, lay your money on the table and then you're free to go. Bear in mind, I'm not stealin',

I'm just collectin' what I would've won if you played poker with me. Come on up. Don't let me have to tell you again."

The startled customers walked quickly to the back of the room and lay their money on the table. Granger and Quentin gathered the money and headed for the door. "Don't no one think of followin' us. If you do, you'll get just what these two got. On second thought, I wish you would follow us. These are the first two people I've killed this week. I'm behind my quota." Quentin laughed at Granger's joking ways. "We'll be easy to find 'cause we're goin' out of town a ways and build a fire to cook our supper. But I can tell you the men from Drippin' Springs who tried that a few days ago are now dead. So y'all come on out and join us at our campsite.

Granger and Quentin left the saloon laughing, mounted their horses, and rode out of town. Some men came out to see which way they had ridden but no one dared follow or challenge them in any way. Granger was still laughing as they rode out of sight.

"Hey, come help me. This marshal's still alive," said one of the saloon patrons. "Come help me get him over to Doc's before he bleeds to death."

Several men carefully carried Marshal Wilson over to the doctor's office and laid him on the exam table. The elderly doctor came out of the back. "What's all the ruckus about?"

"Doc Clements, this marshal got shot over in the saloon after he tried to stop a couple of card cheats."

"What's this man's name?" asked the doctor. The men shook their heads and said they had never seen him before.

"I'm gonna have to stop the bleedin' now and then I've got to get the bullets out. I'm gonna need some help. You men bring me that stack of clean cloths over there. Then somebody go draw water and heat it on the stove until it boils."

The men scampered off to perform their tasks. Doc folded bandages over the bullet holes and ordered several of the men standing around to hold pressure on the holes to stop the blood flow. He counted six entry wounds. But miraculously, they all appeared to have missed vital organs. Wilson had been shot in the left shoulder and left arm. There were bullet wounds to his abdomen but both were far to the side, leaving him to hope he would not have to do abdominal surgery.

The last two wounds were to the marshal's right leg. One of the wounds was in his thigh and it was bleeding profusely. "One of you men cut his pants away. I'm gonna have to get that bullet out of his thigh and stop the bleeding or he's gonna die."

The doctor washed his hands in the basin of hot water that had been brought to him and then began arranging his instruments. He wasted no time in cutting down to the bullet and removing it. When he did, blood spurted from the wound.

"I was afraid of that. The bullet nicked an artery. Hold the cloth in place right here to stop the bleeding while I stitch up the artery." The doctor skillfully and quickly put several small sutures in the damaged vessel.

"Now, slowly release pressure. Let's see if it leaks." As blood flow returned, the doctor smiled as he realized there was no leakage. He quickly sewed up the incision and moved methodically to each of the other bullet wounds. Taking no longer than a minute or so on each one, he selected one of several Tiemann's Bullet Removal Tools, plunged the tool in the wounds, extracted the bullets, and stitched the wounds closed with two or three sutures each.

The doctor noted the color of the marshal and realized he had probably lost too much blood to survive. "Men, that's about all I can do for the marshal. What I know is he's gonna die if I can't get some more blood in him." The doctor paused and rubbed his chin. "There's somethin' called a blood transfusion. They've been used a lot, mainly in big city hospitals. I've never done one but I know it's the only thing that can save him. I've read about them and I think I can do it if I can get one of you men to volunteer to give up some of your blood."

Though none of the men knew the marshal, several stepped forward at once to volunteer. "Sherman, you're the biggest. I guess that also means you have the most blood. You men help me lower the marshal to the floor. Easy. Easy. Now Sherman, get up here on the table."

"Tell me how you're gonna do it, Doc." Sherman tried to sound tough and unafraid but all could tell he was struggling to remain brave.

Doc rummaged around his tray of medical instruments and came away with a tube with a needle at one end and a clamp a couple of inches away. At the other end was another needle. "Sherman, I'm gonna put this needle in your arm and I'm gonna put the other needle in the marshal's arm. Then I'm gonna release the clamp and your blood will flow into the marshal. It won't hurt a bit."

Sherman lay down on the table. "I'm ready, Doc. Let's get this done."

Doc Clements moved closer to Sherman and motioned toward the glass front cabinet on the other side of the room. "One of you men bring me the bottle of whisky."

Sherman looked to where the doctor was directing his command. "Doc, is the whisky for you or for me?"

"Neither one. I want to make sure the needles and your arms are clean." Doc poured some whisky in a small bowl and put the needles inside. Then he put some whisky on a clean cloth and gently rubbed the inside of the elbow of the marshal's arm. He repeated the process with Sherman's arm.

Sherman lay still as the doctor inserted the needle in his arm. "Hey Doc, that didn't hurt at all."

"Lay still, Sherman. I've got to get this needle into the marshal." The doctor loosened the clamp on the hose until blood flowed to the other needle. Then he expertly inserted the needle into the marshal's arm and completely removed the clamp.

Sherman was fascinated by the red tube that was carrying his blood to the marshal who lay a couple of feet below him. "How long will this take, Doc?"

"We'll know in a little while but probably not over thirty minutes. I'll keep monitorin' the marshal to see if there is any change. Look! Already there's more color in his cheeks. And his breathing's gettin' deeper. It's workin'. Sherman you're gonna end up savin' this man's life."

Sherman rested his head back on the table and smiled contentedly. After about fifteen minutes, the doctor reapplied the clamp to the hose and removed the needle from the marshal's arm. He held a clean cloth over the puncture wound. "Somebody hold this on the marshal's arm. I don't want any of the blood we just put in him coming out."

He then removed the needle from Sherman's arm and held a cloth in place. "Now Sherman, I want you to keep this cloth in place and hold your arm up straight. But I want you to continue lying down for half an hour. In fact, why don't you just nod off and take a nap. You're likely to be weak because of the blood you gave the marshal. Now the rest of you, men: Let's get the marshal to the bed in the back room. He'll need to rest up for a day or two before he can move around much."

The men moved the marshal to the bed and the doctor took up residence at his side. "After about thirty minutes, tell Sherman to get up and you let yourselves out. I'm gonna stay with the patient 'til morning."

Directly, the men quietly exited the office as the doctor inspected his patient. He was pleased with the progress he had seen in the brief time since he finished his work. After a couple of hours, the doctor lowered the lamp and lay his head back on his chair. He felt his patient was out of danger but he would remain by his side for the rest of the evening.

When morning came, the doctor was checking the bandage on his patient's leg when the marshal woke up.

"Where am I? I think somebody shot me."

"Just lie still, young feller. You got shot up bad. I thought we were gonna lose you last night. You lost a lot of blood. What's your name?"

"I'm Marshal Junior Wilson from Fredericksburg."

"Pleased to meet you, Marshal. I'm Doc Clements. Most people just call me Doc."

"Thanks for takin' care of me, Doc." He started to sit up.

"Just hold it right there, mister." The doctor put his hand on the marshal's unwounded shoulder and gently urged him to lie back down. "I don't want you messin' up my work. You're not gonna get out of this bed for the next two days. When you're stronger, I'll get some men to move you over to the hotel. But I want you to stay there for at least a week."

"Doc, I know you mean well but I'm on the trail of some outlaws. I can't be laying around like that."

"You'll do what I say or I'll go get the men who brought you in here last night to hold you in bed. You almost died and you need to build up your strength. Those men you're after put six bullets into you. One of those bullets tore the artery in your leg. Even if you feel like you don't need it, you must stay in bed. If you tear the artery, you will bleed out before anyone can even come get me."

Wilson rested back on the bed. "I didn't realize I was that bad off. Thanks, Doc. It sounds like you saved my life."

"I had a little help. You've got about a quart of another man's blood in you. If it hadn't been for him, you'd be dead now."

There was a knock on the front door and a loud whisper. "Hey Doc. It's Sherman. Can I come in?"

"Come on back, Sherman. Our patient's awake."

The big man walked into the bedroom and took off his hat. "How's he doin', Doc?"

"Marshal Wilson, I want you to meet Sherman, the man who saved your life. Sherman, see how much better this man looks with some of your blood in him. But I do notice that he's becomin' almost as ugly as you."

Sherman walked closer to the bed. "Howdy, Marshal. I'm shor glad you're still alive. We thought you were a goner last night."

Wilson extended his hand and Sherman took it. "Thanks for givin' me a bit of your blood. I guess I'm alive because of you."

The big man looked at the floor and shuffled his feet, obviously embarrassed. "Marshal, you can have some more if you need it."

Doc Clements walked back close to the bed. "That's enough talk now. Marshal, you need to rest."

Wilson rubbed his tummy. "I'd rest a bit better if I had somethin' to eat. Can I have some breakfast?"

The doctor smiled. "I'll take that as a sign you're on the road to recovery. Sherman, would you mind goin' over to the café and gettin' our patient some breakfast?"

Sherman was already out the door before the doctor completed his request. In just a few minutes, he came back with a plate of eggs, bacon, fried potatoes, toast, and a cup of coffee. "Sorry, Doc. I should have brought you some coffee. I'll go back and get some."

"That's all right, Sherman. I don't...." But Sherman was already out of the office and running down the street. In a few minutes he came back with a cup of coffee he presented to the doctor.

"Thanks Sherman. I always enjoy coffee in the morning."

The marshal swallowed and looked at Sherman. "I also thank you, Sherman. I've never enjoyed breakfast as much as this. Somehow the food tastes better than any other breakfast I've ever had."

Roy Clinton

CHAPTER 17

On the Road to San Marcos, Texas

B utch Granger could almost feel the noose tightening around his neck. It seemed everywhere he went, he ended up losing his temper and killing people. He knew the Texas Rangers had probably compiled a list of his crimes and were trying to track him down. But what he didn't know is who else might be trailing him.

Rather than traveling in a straight line, he felt he needed to zig zag his way across the state. Otherwise it would be too easy to anticipate his next move. Leaving Bee Caves, Granger and Quentin turned south. He didn't think anyone would think he would head back toward San Antonio.

Granger was also concerned that most of the money he was carrying was gold. He buried all the gold bars from the stagecoach robbery in Stonewall but he was still carrying the gold Double Eagles he got from the couple in Bandera. Granger was worried that paying for liquor and food with gold coins would raise suspicion.

"Quentin, I think it's time we got us some more money."

"But boss, we've got lots of Double Eagles left. Why do we need more money?"

"Don't you think it looks strange when we pay for something using gold coins? Haven't you noticed the way people look at us? We need some foldin' money and some silver."

"But we've got the money from the bank we robbed in Kerrville. Isn't that in your saddlebags?" Quentin knew he was on dangerous ground to either contradict Granger or to question him further.

"Morgan and Skyler had it in their saddlebags."

Quentin wanted to remind Granger he had let the horses go when they were ambushed near Dripping Springs. But he realized to do so would only anger Granger. Quentin felt Granger was planning another bank robbery. But he knew robbing another bank just made them more wanted. "I'm guessin' you're thinkin' on us robbin' a bank. Right?"

"That's where the money is. If we want money, we need to go to a bank." Granger sneered at Quentin and rode on without more explanation for a while. Quentin was hoping Granger would forget about banks and let them concentrate on general stores in small towns. They wouldn't attract that much attention and it would be easier to get out of town.

"We're gonna need some help to take down another bank." Granger was deep into planning their next crime. "I used to ride with a feller who lives in San Marcos. His name's Mike Henson. He's a blacksmith and last I heard he was still there. Tough as they come. We need to go there and get him to join up with us. We can either take the bank there or go down to New Braunfels. Both towns have big banks. I'll bet we can get fifty thousand dollars. Maybe a hundred."

Quentin measured his words carefully. "Why do you think we need someone else?"

"'Cause there will be more people around and we will need another gun in case we have to shoot our way out."

Quentin hated to ask the next question but he felt he needed to know the answer. "Are you plannin' on usin' dynamite?"

Granger turned his sneer to Quentin. "You never know. I've got three sticks left. That'll be enough to get in the safe if we need to open it."

Quentin just nodded his head. He couldn't think of any response that would be well received by Granger. From his perspective, Quentin felt using dynamite alerted people for miles around and made it more difficult to escape. But he knew Granger felt invincible so he would not be concerned with the explosion attracting more attention.

"What if Henson doesn't want to join us?"

Granger sneered and said, "Oh, he'll join us, all right. He owes me. He's just been waitin' for the right opportunity."

Quentin kept riding in silence. He knew it would take them two days to get to San Marcos. Perhaps by then Granger would have changed his mind and they could just lay low for a while. Yet, if they were going to lay low, it would have to be Granger's idea and even then, he knew from experience it wouldn't last long.

Granger seemed to be deep in thought. His silence bothered Quentin. He feared Granger was either hatching some outlandish scheme or was getting ready to explode. "So," Granger began, "tell me why you let Morgan and Skyler put all the bank loot in their saddlebags."

Quentin tried to remember back to that last bank robbery. He knew it was Granger who told them to take the money but he obviously didn't remember doing so. Quentin's pulse quickened and his palms were sweating. "Butch, I seem to remember we swung the money bags from our saddle horns 'til we got out-of-town. Then when we stopped, they just put it all in their saddlebags. They knew yours was full of the Double Eagles and mine was filled with our food and other supplies."

Granger didn't respond but just continued to ride. Quentin began to breathe easier. Maybe he had escaped one of Granger's dangerous explosions.

"We'll go to Du Pre and spend the night tonight. It's a quiet town that has a nice saloon with a hotel and café." Quentin just listened, knowing this was not a discussion but rather an announcement a decision had been made.

* * *

The first people to settle Du Pre came there because of the generous land grants that were being handed out. Each settler was given four thousand, four hundred acres by the Mexican government prior to the Texas Revolution. The town sat between the Indian nations of Karankawas and the Tonkawas and was the site of the Great Raid of 1840, which was the largest Indian raid on cities in the United States.

When Texas was still a republic, thirty-three Comanche chiefs came together to negotiate a peace treaty. Texas officials instead tried to capture them and ended up killing them and their families. The Comanches raised a huge war party and began raids into Southeast Texas, Du Pre being among them.

If Granger knew any of the history of Du Pre, it really didn't matter to him. All that mattered was he would find a place to party and sleep for the night. By dusk, he and Quentin arrived in the town.

As was their practice, they went to the saloon first. A few men were drinking but the thing that caught Granger's eye was a table where three men were playing cards. He got a bottle and two glasses and headed for the table.

"Howdy, gentlemen. Got room for a couple more to join you? I apologize but we were just paid when we finished up working in the stockyards in San Anton and were paid with Double Eagles. We don't have any smaller change." Granger dropped a handful of coins on the table.

The players' eyes grew bigger as they contemplated helping the two strangers part ways with some of their gold. "Shor, we've got room," said one of the men. "And I can make change for you." He swapped one of the gold coins for a few bills and some silver coins.

Nodding toward Quentin, he said, "How 'bout you? Can I give you some change?"

Quentin didn't say anything but pulled a gold coin from his pocket and slid it across the table. The cowboy counted out his change and pocketed the coin. "We're playing a little Five Card Draw. Does that suit you?"

"Works for me," said Granger. "My name is Butch. This here is Quentin."

"Pleased to meet you Butch. Quentin. I'm Jake. This here is Connors. And that is Winston."

Granger and Quentin both nodded at the other men. Jake started dealing and immediately Granger noticed he was dealing from the bottom of the deck. Granger smiled his best sneer and knew he was going to have fun with this man.

"There's a dollar ante and five-dollar limit on bets. Is that too steep for you?"

"That's a might more than we was planning," said Granger. "But I guess it'll do."

Jake smiled a bit and completed his dealing. Each player threw a silver dollar into the pot. "Connors, it's your bet."

"I'll bet three dollars," as he threw his coins into the pot.

Quentin put his three dollars in the pot and said, "Call."

"Call," said Winston and he added to the pot.

"Call," said Granger as he tossed in more coins.

"And I'll call," said Jake as he matched the bet. "Connors, how many cards do you want?"

"I'll take one." Connors discarded one card.

Jake looked at Quentin who said, "I'll take two," as he added his discarded cards.

"Winston?" He held up two fingers to Jake and tossed his discards into the growing pile.

"Granger?"

"I'll take three."

"And the dealer takes three," Jake announced and added his cards to the discard pile. "Your bet, Connors."

"I bet three dollars." Connors added more coins to the pot.

"I'll see your three and raise you three," said Quentin.

"Fold," said Winston.

"Call," said Granger.

"And the dealer calls."

"So, what've you got?" asked Jake. Granger turned over three of a kind. Quentin had two pair. Jake tossed his cards into the discard pile, "Beats me."

"Me too," said Connors.

Granger pulled in the pot. He was sure Jake and probably Connors had better hands. He was also sure Connors was in cahoots with Jake. He didn't know about Winston since he folded.

In the next round Quentin won. Winston won the next pot and then Granger won when Quentin dealt. Over the next several hands Quentin and Granger both won pots and Jake, Connors, and Winston each won smaller pots.

The rest of the customers had departed leaving only the five men playing poker. Granger knew the three men thought they were going to clean up on the two strangers. He knew what was coming next.

"Butch, you and Quentin are doing pretty good. We wanna have a chance to win back some of our money. What do you say if we raise the limit to ten dollars?"

"I guess we could do that. But I know it's gonna be closing time soon. Why don't we just take the limit off?"

Jake grinned and said, "Fine with me. How 'bout you other men?" Quentin just rolled his shoulders indicating he didn't care. Connors and Winston nodded in agreement.

The next several rounds all went to Jake, Connors, and Winston. Even when Granger and Quentin were dealing, the other three always won. After winning the biggest pot of the night, Winston raked in his winnings and said, "Jake, it's your deal. I think I'm headed to bed after this hand."

Jake dealt the hand and Granger once again noticed him dealing from the bottom of the deck. After the first round of betting, Granger noted Connors and Winston both stood pat. Granger pulled his gun and pointed it at Jake.

"I've been watchin' you deal from the bottom of the deck all evening. And I'll just bet Connors or Winston has straight flush and the other has a royal flush."

"Are you callin' me a cheat?" asked Jake.

Granger smiled his widest sneer and said, "Yup. Now Connors and Winston, lay down your hands." As the men complied, Connors revealed a straight flush and Winston showed a royal flush. At that same moment, Jake went for his gun but Granger had anticipated it and pulled the trigger, having already lined up on

Jake's forehead. The other men pulled their guns as Quentin shot Winston and Granger killed Connors. Granger watched as Quentin stretched out his gun toward the bar. As Quentin shot, Granger turned to see the bartender holding a shotgun. Quentin's bullet found its mark on the chest of the bartender. As the man fell, his shotgun went off into the ceiling.

"It's time to collect our winnings," said Granger. "Quentin, go over and get the money from the bartender's cash box. And don't forget to go through his pockets."

Meanwhile, Granger filled his hat with the money from the table and from the pockets of the dead gamblers. "Let that be a lesson to you, men," said Granger as he addressed the corpses at his feet. "Gamblin' is not a good way to make a livin'."

When they got to the door of the saloon, they realized there was no one else in sight. As Granger looked across the street, he saw lamps going out in the hotel and the café. Quentin followed Granger as they walked toward the café. Both men had their guns out.

Suddenly, Granger caught sight of someone with a rifle on the side of the hotel. Before the man could fire, Granger shot him. They continued to the café and opened the door and raised their six-guns.

"Please don't shoot," came a feminine voice from the back. "I won't say a thing about what you've done."

Granger held his gun out and walked toward the voice. "Light a lamp so we can see you." The woman did as she was told. When the room brightened, Granger asked, "Who else is here?"

"It's just me," said the woman. "Please don't hurt me. I've got a little boy and he needs me."

Granger grumbled at her pleading. "All right. But get us some food. We're hungry."

"Yes, sir," said the woman as she raced around the café gathering food for the intruders.

"Where's the marshal of this town?" asked Granger.

"We don't have a marshal. Don't much need one. There hasn't been any crime here before you—I mean in a long time."

"Where's the rest of the men?"

"There's only a few who live in town. The rest are out on their farms or ranches."

She finished fixing their plates, brought them out, and set them at a table for Granger and Quentin. "All I have ready is pork chops, cabbage, and black-eyed peas. And I'll go back and get some cornbread from the kitchen." She returned in a few minutes and placed a skillet of cornbread on the table along with a bowl of butter.

Granger and Quentin were relaxed as they ate. They were in no hurry. Secretly the woman wished they would hurry up and leave town or that some brave men would come in the café and shoot the outlaws. It took fifteen minutes for the men to finish their supper. Both had ordered seconds of everything.

"Now when we leave here, I don't want you tryin' to contact anyone to come after us. If you do, we'll kill 'em just like we did the card cheats in the saloon. And then we'll come back and we'll kill you and your son—all slow like."

The woman shuddered at the threat. "I won't go get anybody to come after you. You have my word on it."

"Swear on your son's life," said Granger.

"I swear," said the woman. "Please just leave us in peace. I won't tell anyone."

Crudder continued south out of Austin, hoping once again to cross paths with Granger and his sidekick. He felt Granger and Quentin's days of freedom were numbered, especially since the Texas Rangers had gotten word across the state to be on the lookout for them. John hoped he would be the one to encounter them first—and soon.

He arrived at the town of Du Pre in the afternoon and rode over to the café. He was looking forward to a good meal. As he swung down from Midnight and tied him to the hitching rail. He noticed five coffins lined up on the boardwalk across the street in front of the saloon. He walked over and watched as two men nailed the lids in place. "What happened here?"

The men regarded Crudder for a moment and then went back to their task without commenting.

"Was this done by men named Granger and Quentin?" The two men exchanged a frightened look but said nothing. Giving up on getting any information, Crudder returned to the café, went inside and got a table.

A very frightened looking woman came to his table. "May I

help you, sir?"

"First, I'd like to know what happened here."

The woman shook her head and began trembling. "I can't say, sir. I'm sorry. I've got a little boy and I can't afford to say anything."

Crudder realized Granger must have threatened her or worse. Once again, he felt his face getting hotter. Granger had to be stopped.

"I'll have just whatever you've got cooked, ma'am."

The woman returned in a few minutes with two fried pork chops, some cabbage, and black-eyed peas. She filled his cup with coffee and went back to the kitchen and retrieved some cornbread and butter.

"Can you at least tell me who did the killin'?"

The woman let out a whimper and shook her head more rapidly. "I can't say anything, mister. Please don't ask me any more questions."

"I'm sorry, ma'am. I know you're frightened. The two men who did this are the worst sort of human beings. I give you my word. I'm gonna find 'em and see that they're brought to justice. Then you won't have to fear 'em any longer."

"Bless you, sir," she said as tears formed in her eyes. She returned to the kitchen as Crudder ate. He could hear her crying in the kitchen. He never saw the woman again and realized she didn't feel safe to come out of the kitchen. When he finished his meal, he left twenty-one dollars on the table. He figured the meal cost a dollar or less but the woman could surely use a little extra to help her and her son.

As Crudder walked out to the hitching rail, he looked up and down the street. The town was very small with only a few buildings. The only people on the street were the two men who were finishing up sealing the coffins. He wasn't sure what had happened but he did know it was the work of Granger and Quentin. And he also knew as bad as things were in Du Pre, they could have been a lot worse.

Roy Clinton

CHAPTER 18

There was simply no way of knowing which way Granger and Quentin were going. Crudder was following the carnage but had no doubt Granger was involved in more crimes than he was discovering. So far, Granger had changed direction multiple times since he left Bandera. All Crudder knew to do now was to continue south hoping to find Granger's trail.

If they were heading south, Crudder knew he was not far behind them. He released tension on the reins and Midnight immediately went into a full gallop. Granger and Quentin could be well ahead of him if they left immediately after their most recent murders. Or they might be in the exact opposite direction.

Midnight ran for several miles when Crudder spotted something that looked out of place. Over to his left, just into a thicket of trees, he saw a thin column of smoke rising beyond the treetops. He slowed Midnight to investigate and found the remains of a campfire. There were no flames but the smoldering ashes let him know someone had been there recently.

He swung down, and surveying the area, he could see where

horses were tied. There were at least two horses that had been hobbled there and perhaps more. He grew more excited when he saw the distinct outline in the tall grass of two sleeping mats. Could it be that Granger and Quentin camped there and just rode out a few minutes before?

He returned to Midnight, mounted him, and let him resume his fast gallop. On the horizon, John could see the dust of a rider. He spoke to Midnight and the mighty horse continued his full out run with no evidence of getting tired.

After a few minutes, Crudder could make out two riders who were moving at a slow trot. One of the riders turned back to see the source of the thundering hooves behind them. John's pulse quickened as he saw the yellow bandana at the neck of the man's black shirt. The man's black hat was pristine. Crudder was sure he was looking at Quentin which meant the rider in front of him was most likely Granger.

Suddenly, John felt something move past his ear and then he heard the report of a gunshot. He reined Midnight in and moved off the road. Crudder knew he missed being shot in the head by only an inch or two.

Quentin and Granger whipped their horses into a gallop. John followed but maintained his distance. He couldn't risk getting closer, for Quentin was obviously a good shot. Quentin reined up behind a rock outcropping. John pulled up, for it looked like Quentin intended to stand and fight. Granger continued galloping ahead. John marveled at the fact Granger had such power that he could get his partner to stop and fight and allow him to escape.

Crudder immediately reined Midnight further off the road and into the trees. As he was swinging down, a bullet struck the ground at his feet. He pulled Midnight deeper into the trees and left him untied in a thicket as he moved ahead on foot. John knew Midnight would remain there and not move until he called or came back for him.

Quentin taunted Crudder. "You're gonna die, cowboy. I don't know who you are but you're gonna die today." Another bullet whizzed by as John started making his way toward Quentin. "Why don't you say somethin', cowboy. Or are you already dead?"

John remained silent. So long as Quentin was talking, John knew exactly where he was. More shots were fired as Quentin tried to locate Crudder. This time the shots were spaced yards apart so John knew Quentin had not seen him moving forward tree by tree.

Quentin continued mocking John. "I don't know if I'm gonna shoot you or gut you like a pig. I kind of like the idea of guttin' you." More shots were fired as John moved ever closer. None of the shots were close to John.

Then, as John moved closer, a twig snapped beneath his feet. Immediately, Quentin zeroed in on his location and put two slugs into the tree Crudder was hiding behind. John recognized Quentin wouldn't need much of an opening to kill him. He also realized Quentin might be the most accurate shot he had come against.

Crudder was close enough he could hear movement from Quentin on the other side of the rocks. John took the opportunity to move closer and go around the side of the outcropping. There was no sound coming from the other side of the rocks. John remained still to see what Quentin's next move would be.

He didn't have to wait long. John heard a horse galloping away so he immediately moved around the outcropping in time to see Quentin getting away. Crudder let out a shrill whistle and Midnight responded by running to John. Quentin got a good head start for Midnight had to navigate through the trees and account for the rocks.

John swung up and gave chase. This time he didn't allow Midnight to run at full gallop. He knew his mighty mount could overtake Quentin quickly. But he wanted to keep at a safe distance for himself and for the sake of Midnight. He wouldn't risk his horse unnecessarily.

Quentin rode hard, occasionally turning back to see if John was closing in. Each time, John reined up just a bit to discourage Quentin from firing any more shots. Quentin was riding in a panic. John figured the reality of Granger abandoning him had sunk in. Granger had saved his own hide but Quentin knew he didn't care if others were sacrificed for the sake of his own safety.

John watched as Quentin left the road. He wasn't sure what he was up to so he kept his distance. Quentin started weaving his way through the trees evidently hoping to lose Crudder. Midnight intuitively continued on the trail of the other horse. John didn't try to guide him around the trees. He knew Midnight would make better time finding his own way.

When Quentin realized his pursuer was staying right with him, he took another tack and headed back toward the road. John felt he needed to close the gap and not take a chance on losing Quentin.

John got closer and then brought Midnight to a stop and pulled his saddle gun from the scabbard. He took careful aim and shot. Quentin's hat hit the ground. John wasn't sure if he hit Quentin or just got his hat. John remained in place and shot twice more in rapid succession.

Quentin's alarm intensified. John could hear him spurring his horse and yelling at him to move faster. Then John heard Quentin let out a groan and hit the ground. In his panic to get away, he caused his horse to cut too close to a tree and Quentin was unseated.

The outlaw rolled on the ground and came up with his six-gun firing directly at Crudder. John stopped and swung down and sent Midnight safely out of the way. John listened to Quentin moving on foot through the trees. His horse had run off and left him. Now Quentin would have to stay and fight or give up. Riding away was no longer an option.

John crept closer—close enough to hear Quentin's labored breathing. Quentin shot again and again. Then John heard the click of the hammer of Quentin's gun falling on a spent cartridge. John made his move before Quentin had a chance to reload. "Drop it now." Crudder was only a few feet from Quentin and his gun was leveled at the fugitive.

Reluctantly Quentin dropped his gun. "So, what do we do now?"

John moved closer to kick Quentin's gun out of the way. "Now I take you in for your many crimes." As John kicked the gun away, Quentin delivered a massive blow with his fist into John's abdomen. The big man put all his weight behind the punch and John sprawled on the ground, his gun flying out of his hand. Quentin quickly kicked John in the ribs before he could regain his composure. The murderer continued kicking John until he was able to roll out of the way so the next kick missed its target.

Crudder got to his feet and closed the distance with Quentin. Quentin swung his fists but he was no match for John in a fist fight. John sidestepped and as Quentin's fist missed its mark, John landed two punches in Quentin's kidney. There was a moan that erupted from the big man but he didn't fall. Instead he threw more wild punches. John dodged and hit Quentin in the abdomen and then in the face. Quentin staggered and came back with another punch that glanced off Crudder's head. John turned and landed another punch in the same kidney he had hit earlier.

Quentin dropped to the ground in pain. "I've had enough, mister. No more." John moved in behind the criminal and pulled him by his collar to his feet. As he was standing up, Quentin reached for the knife he kept sheathed at his waist. "Now I'm gonna cut you, mister."

He took a swing with his knife as John instinctively drew back. The knife nicked John's shirt but didn't connect with his body. Quentin continued swinging wildly back and forth. Each time John would jump backward and remain out of the range of the knife.

"It doesn't look like you're gonna let me take you in."

"You've got that right, cowboy," Quentin growled as he took another mighty swing with the knife.

John pulled the dagger from his sleeve. "Since you're so fond of knives, I guess I'll just use my own. Big man, you're about to meet your Maker."

Quentin jeered at John as he lunged toward the diminutive cowboy. Just as when they had been using fists, John stepped to the side. As Quentin passed by, John took his dagger and plunged it into the outlaw's kidney, quickly withdrew it and stepped back. Quentin straightened and turned toward John and lunged.

This time Crudder plunged his dagger into the big man's abdomen and sunk it to the hilt. Surprise registered on Quentin's face. John pulled the dagger back a bit and thrust it again into his abdomen but this time he turned it up and drove it deeply into Quentin's heart.

John could tell the moment his heart was pierced for Quentin's eyes lost focus and all his resistance faded. The murderer's lifeless body dropped to the ground. John withdrew his dagger and wiped it on the outlaw's fancy yellow bandana.

Once again, John whistled for Midnight. When the horse arrived, John pulled the small shovel from his saddlebag and started digging a grave. As he dug, he reflected on how many times he had used his shovel in that way. Each time he wished it would be the last. But part of him wanted to dig one more grave—this time, for Granger.

With the hole dug, John used his foot to roll Quentin in. He filled the grave and used the flat of the shovel to tamp down the dirt. John removed his hat and bowed his head.

"Well, Lord. Here's another of your errant children. He's a mighty bad man. But you know that already. What I don't understand is why You would let a man like him hurt so many people. But that's all over with now. He's now in your keeping." John paused. "One more thing, Lord. Give me strength to bring his partner to justice."

Crudder clamped on his hat and replaced the shovel in the saddlebag. "Well boy, it looks like we have another ride ahead of us. Are you ready?" Midnight responded with a whinny and nodded his head.

John swung up and continued south toward San Marcos. "Let's go boy. Let's go catch Granger." Midnight went from a walk to a full gallop in just over a second.

CHAPTER 19

San Marcos, Texas

S an Marcos is best known for the beautifully clear San Marcos river that mystifyingly bubbles up out of the ground. The modern city was founded in 1861 but it is considered by many to be the longest inhabited area in the Northern Hemisphere having been the home of people for more than ten thousand years.

John Crudder didn't know where to look for Granger but he was sure he was there. With the rest of his gang wiped out, perhaps he would try to enter an alliance with some other criminal. Maybe he was contemplating other crimes. All John knew for certain was Granger was dangerous and unpredictable. He didn't care who he hurt and appeared to have absolutely no conscience.

As had been his practice in other towns, Crudder went to the marshal's office to see if there was any word about Granger. "Mornin', Marshal." The lawman regarded Crudder for a moment.

"Howdy. How can I help you?"

"My name is Crudder. John Crudder. I used to be the marshal in Bandera." He stuck out his hand and the marshal shook it. "I'm on the trail of Butch 'The Butcher' Granger. He's wanted for murder and bank robbery in at least half a dozen towns."

"Yup, I've heard of him. But he's not here." John noticed the marshal didn't bother to introduce himself. He had a feeling he was going to have a brief visit.

"Beggin' your pardon, Marshal, but how can you be so sure he's not here?"

"'Cause I make it my business to know what's goin' on in my town. If he was here, I'd know it."

"I see. Well I'm glad to hear that. Anyway, I trailed him here and lost him about an hour ago." Crudder felt it was best not to talk about the death of Quentin. "A few nights ago, he murdered five people in Du Pre. He and his gang murdered Marshal Atkins of Dripping Springs. All total he has murdered twenty-five to thirty people, maybe more."

"Well, it makes me really glad he's not here. We don't need his kind around here. Thanks for stoppin' by, Mr. Crudder. Now I need to get back to work."

John was baffled at the marshal's response. As he walked out of the office, there were several shots being fired. John ran toward the gunfire and was closely followed by the marshal. A clerk ran out of the bank yelling, "Marshal, Marshal! Somebody just robbed the bank!" The marshal ran toward the bank followed by Crudder.

"Slow down, Pete. Tell me what happened."

"A man came in the bank. He had sort of a weird smile on his face. I asked if I could help him but he just smiled at me. Then he pulled out his gun and said, 'Give me all the money.' I didn't know what to do so I gave him the money from the box beneath my window. I think it was a little over a hundred dollars."

Crudder turned and started to run back to the marshal's office to get Midnight. "Just wait a minute, Mr. Crudder. You're not a lawman. You're not goin' after him."

"But Marshal. The description matches Granger. He always has a sneer on his face. The longer we wait, the greater chance that he'll get away."

"I said you're not goin' anywhere." Crudder was infuriated that the marshal didn't have a sense of urgency about capturing such an malevolent man.

The marshal turned again to the bank clerk. "Now, Pete, what was all the shootin' about?"

"Oh, yeah. Just before he took the money, he shot twice into the ceiling and said if any one came after him, he would shoot 'em. Then he asked me how far it was to Martindale."

A crowd had gathered around the marshal in front of the bank to see what the shooting was about. The marshal seemed to enjoy being in the center of attention and being able to control the conversation. "Now, Pete, how many men did he have with him?"

"There was just him. I've never been in a bank robbery before. I thought there was always a gang that held up banks."

"After he asked how far it was to Martindale, what happened next?" John couldn't believe the questions the marshal was asking.

What did it matter? What mattered was getting after Granger just as soon as possible.

"Well, I guess that was about it. He scared me so bad I…." The clerk leaned in to the marshal and whispered, "I almost wet my pants."

"Now just one more thing," said the marshal in a voice loud enough for the assembled crowd to hear his questions. "I got here right after the shots were fired. I didn't see anyone come out of the bank."

"He didn't go out the front door. He went out the back. In fact, that's how he got in. That puzzles me 'cause we keep the back door locked."

The marshal thought about it for a moment. "He either had a key, or he picked the lock. Or Pete, you forgot to lock the door when you came to work."

"I did no such thing, Marshal. I've worked her nigh onto ten years and I've never left the back door unlocked."

"It don't matter none, Pete. I wasn't accusin' you of nothin'. There is one more thing. Did you see what color horse he was ridin'?"

"No, Marshal. I was too scared to go out back. What if he was standin' there waitin' to shoot me?"

The marshal turned and addressed the assembled crowd. "Now, men, I want ten of you to be on a posse. We won't be gone long. We're gonna ride over to Martindale and bring this hombre back. We should be back by supper."

Crudder stepped forward. "Marshal, do you mind if I go now?"

"You can leave, just as long as you don't go toward Martindale. You're not on this posse."

"I give you my word, I'll not go to Martindale." John knew Granger had never tipped his hand about the direction of his travel. He was certain he was continuing south. It seemed to John the marshal's only interest was showing off in front of the crowd and hoped he wouldn't have to encounter Granger.

Crudder went back to the marshal's office and swung up onto Midnight. He turned south and trotted until the edge of town. Then he allowed Midnight to go into a full gallop as he headed to New Braunfels.

Roy Clinton

CHAPTER 20

New Braunfels, Texas

J ohn rode hard all the way to New Braunfels, with a couple of short breaks when they crossed streams. Midnight galloped effortlessly. John was angry the marshal in San Marcos had delayed him so much. He knew he could have easily caught Granger if he been allowed to leave immediately. Now, he knew it was possible for Granger to pull off the road and hide and perhaps get away.

When Midnight was watered and refreshed, they resumed their journey. This time John urged Midnight to run even harder. The great horse complied unleashing an even greater burst of speed.

Crudder estimated he had traveled around eighteen miles when he saw a cloud of dust ahead. They were nearing New Braunfels and John knew it would only be another mile or two before they arrived in town. John couldn't make out the source of the dust cloud but knew it was Granger riding as fast as possible. If he didn't catch him before he arrived in town, John knew he might be able to blend in with the town folk making him harder to capture.

Midnight was closing the distance on the other horse but John could still not see anything but a cloud of dust. He wondered if Granger had seen him, although he didn't think that was possible. The road was dry so the dust cloud was thick. As much as John didn't want to do it, he knew he had to slow down. He couldn't see the road ahead and, looking down, realized he could not even see Midnight's hooves. As much as he wanted to catch Granger, he wouldn't risk his horse to do so. After a few minutes, reluctantly, he reined Midnight in and adopted a gentle lope for the rest of the journey.

A few minutes later, Crudder arrived on the outskirts of New Braunfels. Crossing the bridge over the Guadalupe River, John pulled Midnight under the bridge to let him get some more water. He was sure the dusty ride had taken a toll on his horse. Midnight drank and then started coughing. He would hold his head up and then cough some more. John had never heard Midnight cough repeatedly. On the rare occasions he did cough, he would cough a single time.

John swung down and loosened the saddle girth to allow Midnight to get deeper breaths. The mighty horse continued to cough and try to clear the dust from his lungs. John regretted having Midnight run into the dust cloud. He was determined to catch Granger but not at the sacrifice of his horse.

The urgency with which John was chasing Granger was gone. All that mattered now was Midnight's health. After letting his horse rest for about fifteen minutes, John led Midnight up from the river and back to the road. Instead of riding, Crudder thought it best that he walk his horse on into town. As they walked, Midnight continued coughing.

When he got into town, John decided he would look for a veterinarian just to make sure Midnight was all right. Not seeing any sign for a vet, John took Midnight to the livery stable.

"Howdy, mister," said the stableman.

"Mornin'," replied Crudder. "I wonder if you could tell me if there's a veterinarian in town?" As if on cue, Midnight resumed coughing.

"Sounds like you've got a sick horse, mister. Doc Shriver's out checkin' on a horse right now but he should be back soon. He don't have no office. He just comes here when there's a need."

"Do you have any idea how long he'll be gone?"

"No, but it shouldn't be long. He's—well look at that. Here he comes now. Hey, Doc. You've got a customer here." The doctor swung down from his horse and tied him at the hitching rail.

"Now which one of you needs a doctor?" asked the veterinarian with a smile.

Midnight started coughing again. "Doc, my horse just started this coughing a few minutes ago. Can you see what's wrong with him?"

"Young man, I can see what's the matter with him from here. You blame fool, looks like you rode him into a dust storm. But there hasn't been any dust blowing around here today. Look at him. He's all covered in dust. The same is true for you. Take off your hat and look at it."

John removed his hat. Though he knew it was normally black, it had so much dust on it that it appeared to be grey. The doctor moved closer to Midnight and pulled back the horse's lips. He then examined Midnight's nostrils.

"Son, your horse will probably develop pneumonia. Specifically, he'll develop aspiration pneumonia. There's not a lot you can do for him at this point other than get your saddle off him. You're not gonna be able to ride him for a week. Maybe longer. In fact, I have known some horses not to be completely over pneumonia for as long as a year. He needs to rest and breathe fresh air. How did you get him in a dust cloud?"

"Well, Doc. I was ridin' behind someone who was kickin' up a lot of dust."

"From the looks of it, you must have been ridin' hard. He's swallowed a lot of dust. Actually, what he's swallowed doesn't matter that much. But he's breathed in more dust than he should have. Did you catch whoever you were chasin'?"

"No, I didn't. When I realized how thick the dust was, I slowed down so we would get out of the dust. But to be honest, Doc, the reason I slowed down was I couldn't see Midnight's hooves. I didn't even think about the dust he was breathing until he started coughin'."

"I'm glad you slowed down. How long was he breathin' the dust?"

"Probably ten or fifteen minutes."

"Well, the damage is done. All we can do now is wait for him to get better."

John felt horrible because he knew Midnight's cough and coming pneumonia was preventable. "Doc, what's gonna happen to Midnight?"

"I have to be frank with you, son. Your horse could die. I don't think he will but pneumonia is a serious condition. However, in this case, we've caught it before it turns into pneumonia so he's got a better chance."

John wanted to find out all he could about his horse's illness. "Doc, you said he would develop aspiration pneumonia. I've never heard of that."

"That happens when an animal, in this case your horse, ingests a foreign object into his lungs. For him, the foreign objects are millions of particles of dirt. Pneumonia is a natural response to that. His body will try to throw off the dust. His lungs are able to pull out the air he needs to breathe. The dust has clogged them up. By this evening, your horse's breath will start smelling sweet. By mornin', if not before, he'll be runnin' a fever."

John rubbed Midnight's neck. "Is there anything we can do for him now?"

The vet opened his leather bag. "I've got medicine that will help. If you assist me, I want to get your horse to drink this whole bottle. Hold his head high and I'll put it just inside his lips. He should swallow it." John did as instructed and Midnight drank down the medicine. "That should keep your horse from gettin' too sick. I'm hopin' his fever will not get high. With any luck, he'll recover quickly. But as I said earlier, pneumonia is a serious condition. You need to prepare yourself for any outcome. He could get a lot worse."

John knew he was helpless to do anything to help Midnight at this point. He felt great sadness knowing his recklessness had caused the problem. He extended his hand to the doctor. "My name's John Crudder. And my horse is Midnight."

The doctor shook his hand. "I'm Doc Shriver and I'm pleased to meet you both. This sure is a fine animal. Is he a thoroughbred?"

"Yes, he is. I bought him in New York City a few years ago and brought him to Colorado by train and then rode him down to Texas. He's an amazing horse. Doc, I know it sounds crazy but sometimes, I think he understands me when I talk to him." Midnight whinnied and nodded his head up and down.

The doctor laughed. "He may be the most beautiful horse I've ever seen. I don't see many thoroughbreds around here though I did see a good many back in Philadelphia."

"How long were you in Philadelphia?" asked John.

"I grew up there and then attended the Philadelphia Veterinary College soon after it opened in '52. Then after graduation, I came out west and eventually got here. I guess I've been here in New Braunfels now for about fifteen years."

"I'm sure glad you were here." John paused and looked at his boots before continuing. "I don't know what I'd do if something happened to Midnight."

The doctor put his hand on John's shoulder. "I hope he's gonna be fine. Let's just allow him to rest and not do anything to bring him any additional stress. In fact, I don't think it will be a good idea for you to be around him for long periods each day. I've already seen how he responds to you. He wants to please you so your presence may actually be bringing him greater stress."

"I certainly don't want to make it harder on him. I guess I'll just find something else to occupy my time and stay away from Midnight as much as I can."

"Well, I wouldn't go that far. Just limit your visits with him to twice a day for no more than thirty minutes each time."

John nodded his head in agreement. "I can do that. How much do I owe you?"

"Let's talk about that later. If you like, I'll check on him several times each day since I'm around the stables most of the time."

"That would be great, Doc. If anything happens, please let me know. I guess I'll be staying in a hotel in town."

The stableman spoke up. "Kramer's Kitchen and Hotel, right across the street, has good food and clean sheets."

"Then that's where I'll be stayin'. Thanks Mister…."

"Name's Austin on account of where my parents lived when I was born." Then with a twinkle in his eye, he added, "I'm shor glad I wasn't born in New Braunfels." The stable keeper grinned and stuck out his hand.

"Thanks, Austin. I appreciate you takin' care of my horse. If you don't mind, I'll drop by several times a day just to ask how Midnight's doin'. I'll not come in so he can see me but I would like to ask you to check on him for me. And I'm glad to pay you for the extra trouble."

"It ain't no extra trouble. All you'll owe me is for his stall and feed."

John looked at the doctor. "Would it be all right if I gave him a good brushin' before I go?"

"John, why don't you let Austin do that? As I was sayin', Midnight wants to please you. The more you're around here, the more stress he'll have and the slower he'll heal."

"I guess that will be fine, Doc. Thanks for the reminder. And Austin, I'd thank you to brush him a bit if it's not too much trouble."

"Ain't no trouble at all."

John tipped his hat and walked across the street to the hotel. He paid for a room for a week. He was tempted to only get the room for a couple of nights but he wanted to do exactly what the doctor said. It would be difficult for him not to continually check in on Midnight but he was determined to follow the doctor's orders.

Crudder accepted the fact that he had lost Granger's trail and that he was going to be confined to New Braunfels for the next week or longer. After paying for his room he went into the dining room. It was small but clean. The tables were painted red and white in a checkerboard pattern that gave them the look of being covered with fine tablecloths. Short white curtains were over the tops of the windows. The room was bathed in the reflected sunlight.

John looked at a menu board in the front of the dining room. When the waitress arrived, he made his selection. "I think I'll have the meatloaf. Is it good? I've only had it one other time."

"It's delicious. I would also recommend the macaroni pudding."

"I've heard about it but never tried it. Is it a dessert?"

"No, it's macaroni, cheese, a little onion, and a little milk."

"That sounds good. You know, I remember hearing Thomas Jefferson ate it in Italy and then brought the recipe back to Virginia."

The waitress looked a bit sad. "I always thought my mother was the first to make it."

John was quick to respond. "Well, she probably was. Maybe what Jefferson brought back from Italy was some other dish."

The waitress walked away a bit crestfallen. John wished he had not repeated something he had picked up when he was attending Harvard. Sometimes it's better to keep one's mouth shut.

When the food came, John thanked the waitress and dug in. After a few minutes, she came by to see if he needed anything else. "This meal is delicious. My compliments to the chef."

"We don't have a chef. Just my mom doing the cooking." Once again, John realized he had stuck his foot in his mouth.

"My apologies. I just meant I love your mom's cookin'. When I'm finished, I'd like to go back to the kitchen and tell her. That is, if that's all right."

The waitress smiled. "Yes, that'll be all right."

"My name's John. What's your name?"

"My name is Charlotte. Pleased to meet you, John." John registered a bit of shock as he heard the name. "Did I say something wrong, mister?"

"No. I'm sorry. I was just surprised at your name. My wife's name is Charlotte. This is the first time I've met anyone else with that name. Well, Charlotte, you have a lovely name."

She smiled and headed back toward the kitchen. In a few moments, John saw the kitchen door open just a crack. He thought he could see two heads trying to sneak a peek at the diner who was from out-of-town. John continued eating and tried to act as though he had not seen the ladies looking at him.

When his meal was finished, he put his napkin on the table and went to the kitchen door and knocked lightly. John could hear Charlotte giggle. After a few seconds, Charlotte opened the door and said, "Yes?"

"Hello Miss Charlotte, I'd like to compliment the cook—I mean your mother—on the fine meal."

An older woman replaced Charlotte and opened the door wide. "Yes, may I help you?"

John cleared his throat. "Ma'am, my name is John and I'll probably be eatin' here a lot for the next week. I just wanted to say that your meatloaf and macaroni puddin' was the best I've ever had."

"Thank you, John. My name is Naomi. I'm Charlotte's mom." She wiped her hands on her apron and extended one to John. He shook it while holding his hat in his other hand. "I understand your wife is also named Charlotte."

"That's right, ma'am. In fact, I've never met anyone else with that name before meetin' your daughter. Anyway, ma'am, I just wanted to say how much I've enjoyed the meal."

"I'm glad, John. You said you are staying for a week. Are you staying in our hotel?"

"Yes, ma'am. I registered a few minutes ago."

"Then you've already met my husband. His name's Homer. John, if you'd like, we can just keep track of your meal charges and add them to your hotel bill."

"Yes, ma'am. That would be fine. I appreciate you doin' that." John wasn't sure what to say next or how to extract himself from the conversation. "Well, I guess I better be goin'. Thanks again for the fine meal."

"You're welcome, John."

As John walked out of the dining room, he wondered how he would spend his time while he was in New Braunfels. He wished he knew where Granger had gone. Most likely he had made his way on toward San Anton. By the time John and Midnight were able to travel, Granger could be anywhere.

John was clear that the most important thing he could do now was to take care of Midnight. Crudder walked back across the street and found the stable keeper leaning back in a chair at the front of the livery whittling. "Hello, Austin." John heard Midnight whinny.

Austin held a finger up to his mouth indicating John should be quieter. John nodded his head in response. This time he whispered. "How's he doing?"

"Fine," said Austin. "No real change."

John mouthed, "Thank you" but little sound came out. He waved at Austin and walked back across the street. Crudder felt like a fish out of water. First, he insults the waitress. Now, he can't even follow the simplest instructions not to disturb Midnight. Then to top it all off, he was destined to spend the next week with nothing to do other than hope time would pass quickly.

Crudder walked down West San Antonio Street until he got to the Comal River. He stood and looked at the crystal-clear water and thought it was even clearer than the Medina that ran in front of his home in Bandera. John picked up some pebbles and tossed them in the river and then walked back up San Antonio Street.

When he got to Castell Street, he saw a large church off to the right. He turned down the street and walked to the church. The sign out front said:

The Church of
Saints Peter and Paul

John marveled at the building. It looked like it had just been built. It was constructed of limestone that John supposed had been quarried nearby. He removed his hat and walked inside.

"Hello, my son," said the priest. "I don't remember seeing you here before. Are you new to this area?"

"Hello, father. No, I don't live here. I'm just in town for a week."

"I see. Are you Catholic?"

"No, sir. I guess I'm Methodist. At least I've been to a Methodist church a few times."

"All of God's children are welcome here. I'm Father Hernandez."

"Pleased to meet you, Father. My name is John Crudder."

"And I'm pleased to meet you, my son. Feel free to come in and look around. Or you may sit and pray. And if you want to talk, I'm always willing to listen."

"Thanks, father. I guess I'll just look around. It looks like the church is new."

"Actually, we have had a church here since the mid-forties. But you're right about this building. It is only three years old."

"Well, it's beautiful, padre."

"You said you'll be in town for a week. Do you mind me asking why you're here?"

"Father, I ran my horse into a thick dust cloud and now he's sick."

"That sounds very sad. Would you like to talk about it?" The priest motioned to a pew and he slid in. John moved in beside him.

"I was chasin' a bad man and his horse was stirring up a lot of dust. Instead of me bein' concerned about my horse breathing all the dust, I rode ahead. He got so much dust that he started coughing. The vet here said he was gonna develop pneumonia. He said he would need at least a week to get better. But he also said…he said…he could even die." John's eyes filled with tears. He was surprised by the emotion he was feeling.

The priest listened as John spoke and nodded his head. "I can see that makes you very sad. It doesn't sound like you harmed your horse on purpose."

"No, I didn't, Father, but the fact remains I did hurt him." John wiped the tears from his eyes. "I don't know what I would do if somethin' happened to him."

"I will pray for your horse, John. I trust he'll recover very soon. John, you said you were chasing a bad man."

"That's right, father. A man named Granger murdered an old man and woman in Bandera. I've been chasing him for the past few weeks. He's killed many more people since then. Some, he blew up in a stagecoach. Several ladies and a baby were among the dead."

The priest crossed himself. "Dear God. How is it possible for someone to be so wicked?"

"I wonder the same thing, padre. I used to be a lawman so I've been around a lot of evil people but I've never known of anyone like Granger. He doesn't have a conscience."

"Maybe he has a conscience but he's not able to listen to it any more. Saint Paul wrote to a young man named Timothy and said someday there would be people who have seared their conscience. This man named Granger sounds like that's what happened to him."

"I don't know about that, padre. What I do know is he kills people and doesn't feel anything. He's pure evil."

"You said you used to be a lawman. May I ask you what you're going to do when you catch him?"

"I don't know, padre. I'll try to take him into custody and deliver him to San Anton. That's where he's to stand trial first. But I must admit, I'd just like to kill him."

The priest crossed himself again. "Vengeance is mine; I will repay, saith the Lord."

"I believe that, Father. But I also know Granger may not leave me any choice. I've already had to kill the men who were ridin' with him. If I hadn't, they would have killed me or killed other people."

The priest continued listening and nodded his head. "I hope you're able to take him to jail in San Antonio. Do you have any idea where he is now?"

"No. I lost him as I was ridin' into New Braunfels. He's likely gone on to San Anton. But since he's wanted there, he may have bypassed the city and gone on to Mexico."

The priest paused, deep in thought. "John, does your conscience ever bother you for the people you've killed?"

John thought for a moment. "Padre, this is hard to say but no. My conscience doesn't bother me. Now I wished I hadn't had to kill most of 'em. But I never killed a person who didn't deserve it or give me any other choice."

Once again, the priest paused. Then looked back at John. "Do you think there's any possibility Granger is still in New Braunfels?"

John was startled by the question. "I don't know, Father. I was sure he kept runnin' south. But it's possible he's still here. I don't know why I never considered that." John stood abruptly. "Padre, thanks for listenin' to me talk. I appreciate that. Now, I've got to go. Granger may be right here nearby. I have to find him."

Roy Clinton

CHAPTER 21

Crudder walked out of the church and went back down Castell Street. When he got to San Antonio Street, he turned right. His eyes focused on every window in every building he passed. He subconsciously lifted his six-gun from his holster about an inch and then dropped it back into place. It would not do for him to face Granger and have his gun stuck in his holster.

Could Granger still be here? The answer staring him in the face was—*absolutely*. How could he have missed that possibility? Because his focus was on Midnight and on his thoughtlessness in getting him injured. But the question as to where Granger could be hiding in New Braunfels still eluded him.

At the edge of town, John turned around and came up the other side of San Antonio Street, being careful once again to look for anyone and anything that could be out of place. Nothing out of the ordinary caught his eye. Dusk was near. He knew the veterinarian had said he could have thirty minutes with Midnight so he intended to take every minute of it.

The livery stable was on Seguin Street. At the corner of San Antonio and Seguin stood a large park-like square. Individuals and families were enjoying the open space. Crudder slowed his pace and took in details of each man who might fit Granger's description. In particular, he was looking for a man with ears that stuck out giving him the appearance of an elf, a large stomach, unshaven, causing his face to look dirty, wearing wide suspenders.

No one fit the description so John turned right on Seguin and walked toward the livery. Every window held the promise of finding Granger. Yet, the absence of men fitting his description brought disappointment.

Arriving at the livery, John started whistling. He was greeted by a whinny from Midnight who recognized his master even though he could not yet see him. Austin was sitting in the same place whittling. "Evening, John."

"Hello again, Austin. How's our patient?"

"The doc confirmed he does have pneumonia but was not concerned since he was expecting that. Your horse is running a fever and you can smell his breath. It has that sweet smell the doc said to expect."

John walked back to Midnight and spoke softly to him. Midnight nodded his head up and down in response to John's gentle voice and stroking his neck. "Thanks for takin' good care of him, Austin. It has been hard for me to stay away but I knew you were seeing after his needs."

"You're welcome, John. Actually, the doc didn't act too concerned. He said even though Midnight had pneumonia, he felt it was gonna be a light case that would last only a week or so."

John was both encouraged and disheartened by the news. He was glad his horse was doing better than expected but he remembered the doc saying Midnight couldn't be ridden for at least a week. Now hearing it would be "a week or so" dampened his spirits.

John looked back at Austin. "How's his appetite? Did he eat any oats?"

"He shor did. He was powerful hungry. I gave him a bucket and he ate it purdy quick. I could tell he wanted more but I'm not gonna let a horse I'm lookin' after get foundered."

"Thanks for that, Austin. He's always had a good appetite." John continued rubbing Midnight and then addressed Austin again. "When I rode in this mornin', I had been chasin' a man. Did anyone come in here on a horse that had been rode hard and maybe was even lathered up?"

"Shor did. He was a big guy, looked like he was grinnin' but then I realized that was just the way his face was. He had those sticky-outie ears. I thought he was a no-account man for ridin' his horse as hard as he did."

John's face brightened. "Is his horse still here?"

"That horse is but he traded me for another horse about an hour ago. He hasn't been gone from here long. Does that sound like the man you were chasin'?"

"That's him. Austin, I need another horse I can ride. Do you have one I can use for a while? I'll pay you whatever you want.

"Well, I don't generally rent horses but I've got a couple for sale. If you want to buy one, you can use it as long as you want and then we can talk about me buyin' it back."

John looked through the stalls and spotted a horse he liked. "How 'bout that chestnut stud. Is he for sale?"

"Shor is. You've got an eye for horseflesh. He's the best of the lot. I'll take two hundred for him. But he's worth more."

John pulled the money out of his pocket. "Austin, will you put my saddle and bridle on him? I need to get some food at Kramer's." Crudder was already running out of the livery.

He spotted the waitress immediately and she headed over to John. Before she could speak, John started placing an order. "Charlotte, I've got to leave in a few minutes. Do you think you can get me enough food to eat on the trail for about two days?"

"Yes, sir, I can do that. The special tonight is pork chops. But I've also got some ham and momma just pulled out a pan of biscuits."

"That sounds fine. Please put it on my bill and I'll be back in a few minutes to pick it up." John went to the room he had rented for the week and picked up his saddlebags, bedroll, and rifle and then ran back to the livery. Austin was leading the chestnut out to the front of the stable.

John put his gear on the saddle and then ran across the street to get his food. Charlotte had it packaged to go in his saddlebags but she kept out two biscuits with thick slices of ham in each and put them in a little cloth sack. He quickly added the food to his saddlebags but tied the little cloth sack to his saddle   horn.

Waving to Charlotte and Austin, John swung up and loped the

chestnut down Seguin to San Antonio Street and turned left. After a couple of minutes, he was clear of buildings so he urged his horse to gallop. He found he had to kick with both feet and make exaggerated movement with the reins to get the horse to run. Oh, how he missed Midnight!

John had only traveled about a mile when he slowed his horse. It was getting too dark to run. But his plan was to keep riding hoping to spot a campfire somewhere out-of-town. Crudder hoped he had guessed right and Granger was still headed south. The chestnut seemed surefooted and was willing to continue walking in nearly total darkness. The moon was rising but John could see it was far less than full. It would, however, provide some additional light when it came up.

He took the opportunity to eat one of the ham biscuits the waitress had made for him. The food was good but his only interest was in getting enough nourishment to fuel his pursuit of Granger. Crudder continued riding and had been on the trail for more than an hour when he spotted a campfire off to the left of the road in a stand of trees.

John carefully moved his horse well away from the campfire and tied him on a long lead so he could graze. He wasn't sure it was Granger but he had to assume it was until he was convinced otherwise. Lacking a better plan, he intended to sneak up on Granger and perform a citizen's arrest.

Crudder tied his horse, got his saddle gun, and slowly moved toward the campsite using trees for cover. When he got close enough to make out a figure sitting by the fire, he couldn't tell if it was Granger or not. John was determined not to get in a hurry and force a gunfight in the dark. He wanted to take Granger alive so he could stand trial for his crimes.

Ever so slowly, John moved toward the fire. He would take a step, stop and listen, keeping watch on the figure sitting by the fire. The man was eating and it sounded like he was humming to himself. John got right up to the man without being heard. The man's humming had no doubt contributed to Crudder's stealthy approach.

John was finally right behind the man. He firmly pushed the barrel of his gun into the man's back. "Granger, this is the end of the line for you. Put your hands up or I'll take great pleasure in shooting you where you sit."

The man's hands went up and John moved around so he could get a look at the man's face. "I don't know who you're after mister but you've got the wrong man." But Crudder saw the description he was given fit perfectly. Granger's mouth was pulled back exposing his teeth so it looked like he was smiling. His ears stuck out prominently and wide suspenders covered his huge belly. f

"You're exactly who I'm lookin' for, Granger. Now reach down with your left hand and slip your gun from the holster and toss it over here." Granger did as he was ordered. "Now I want you to lie on your stomach and put your hands behind your back." Granger put his big belly on the ground and held his arms out by his side.

"I can't get my hands behind my back, mister. This is the best I can do." John spotted a coil of rope on Granger's saddle. He stepped over to retrieve it, keeping his rifle trained on Granger the whole time. As John knelt to tie his hands, Granger made his move. He flipped his body over with greater agility than John thought possible and used his legs to knock Crudder down.

John scrambled trying unsuccessfully to get his feet under him when Granger unleashed a violent kick into his ribs. John realized his ribs still hurt from where Quentin had kicked him. Granger pressed his advantage by kicking John again. Crudder found it difficult to breathe. The Butcher must have broken some of his ribs and knocked the breath out of him. Granger pulled his leg back to kick him again but Crudder had rolled away so the kick only connected with air and left Granger off balance.

John struggled to his feet as Granger regained his balance. The big man lunged but John was able to easily sidestep the attack. As Granger went by, John landed a solid punch into Granger's gut but the hulking figure seemed unfazed. As he turned toward John, John unleashed a flurry of punches to Granger's face. Blood flowed from his nose and from a cut above his eye but Granger didn't seem to be hurt.

As John prepared for the next attack, he saw Granger pick up the gun he had tossed to the side. Without waiting to see what Granger was going to do, John picked up his rifle and brought the butt down heavily on Granger's forehead. The big man just stared up at John and continued moving the six-gun into position. John used all his strength to bring the butt of the saddle gun down on Granger's forehead again.

This time, Granger went down and didn't move. John quickly moved to get the rope and tie Granger's hands and feet. Then he ran back to where his horse was tied and quickly rode to the campfire. John removed the handcuffs from his saddlebag and cuffed Granger's hands behind his back. He then tied the cuffs to the rope and pulled Granger's feet up behind him in a hog tie.

By the time Granger regained consciousness, John was eating his other ham biscuit and drinking Granger's coffee. "Why'd you go and hit me so hard?" Then Granger, realizing how he was tied, bellowed loudly. "You can't truss me up like a pig. I ain't no animal."

John continued eating his supper and ignored Granger. "Hey you! I'm talkin' to you. You better untie me or you're gonna be sorry." Crudder finished his biscuit and set down his coffee cup. He stood up and went over to Granger and kicked him as hard as he could in the ribs. Granger let out a yell. Crudder stepped back a couple of steps and then ran forward and unleashed another powerful kick into the outlaw's ribs.

Granger yelled out in pain. "Why'd you go and do that, mister? I ain't done nothin' to you."

"Actually, you kicked me twice in the same place I just kicked you. In the mornin', we're gonna take a little trip to San Anton. I don't want the trip to be too comfortable for you. I'm hoping I broke a couple of your ribs so you won't be inclined to give me trouble on our trip."

"Why are we goin, to San Anton? There ain't no reason to go there."

"I'm takin' you there to stand trial for murder. And that will be the first of several trials. Granger, you have murdered men, women, and children without remorse. Now, you're gonna get to pay for your crimes. I am gonna enjoy watchin' you hang."

"Ain't nobody hangin' me." Granger pulled against his restraints. "You just let me up from here and I'll show you…" Granger stopped talking as Crudder stood up over the man. "No, please, mister. Don't kick me no more. I ain't gonna cause you problems."

John sat back down and picked up his coffee cup, contentedly finished it and poured himself another. He then put down his ground cloth and rolled out his bedroll. Granger didn't make another sound that night.

✻ ✻ ✻

At first light, Crudder got up and rekindled the fire. He was grateful his ribs were just a bit sore and didn't appear to be broken. John heated the coffee and ate two of the cold pork chops the waitress had prepared for him. They were delicious. He finished his coffee, had a couple of biscuits, and saddled both horses.

John untied Granger's feet and took him a pork chop. Granger tore into it as Crudder held it close to his mouth. It only took a few seconds for him to devour it. "I want another one and I want some coffee."

Crudder held Granger's canteen up so he could get a drink. "Where's the rest of my breakfast? I want some coffee." John ignored him and used his boot to knock down the flames of the fire and then poured the rest of the coffee over the coals. "Hey, you.

That was my coffee. You can't treat me like an animal."

John wanted to tell Granger what an animal he was and that was exactly how he should be treated. But he knew it wouldn't take much for John to let his anger build to the point where he was willing to end Granger's life.

Crudder helped the big man up and took him over to his horse. "I can't get on the horse with my hands behind my back. You've got to let me loose if you expect me to ride." John said nothing but took out his six-gun and pointed to the saddle. The big man lifted his foot toward the stirrup and John moved in to help him. But in that instant, Granger turned around and used his head as a battering ram and struck John on the bridge of his nose. Immediately blood began to flow. John backed up a step and brought the butt of his pistol down on Granger's nose, reopening the wound he had put there the night before.

"Shoot me! Just shoot me." Granger shouted at John. Then his angry barks turned to pleading. "I don't want to hang. Please mister, just shoot me."

John pointed to the saddle and once again the big man raised his leg to the stirrup. This time he didn't offer any resistance as John moved forward to boost the man into the saddle. John listened as Granger's whimpers became a soft cry. For the first time since he started tracking Granger, he was glad he hadn't killed the brutal man. It seemed his anticipation of hanging was greater than his fear of dying.

CHAPTER 22

San Antonio, Texas

By late in the afternoon, John and Granger arrived in San Antonio. John could tell Granger was in pain from his injured ribs. As they rode slowly down Broadway Street, John saw people stare and point at the prisoner. Crudder wondered if any of them recognized Granger or if they were just fascinated with the sight of the handcuffed man being brought into town.

It didn't take John long to find the marshal's office. Word had already traveled ahead, for the marshal was waiting in front of his office when John arrived.

"Well, you got Granger. Climb down, mister. I'm shor glad to make your acquaintance. I'm Marshal Dobbin. John Dobbin."

"Howdy, Marshal. My name is Crudder. John Crudder. I can see you already know who's gonna be the guest in your jail."

Crudder helped the marshal get Granger off his horse and into the jail. Over the next hour, John filled the marshal in on the string of crimes he knew of as he chased Granger across the state. The marshal kept careful notes and said he would get word to Texas Rangers so they would know of Granger's capture and of the other crimes he had committed.

"Howdy, Marshal." A large black man walked into the office.

"Howdy, Judge. I want you to meet John Crudder. John, this is Judge William A. Price."

"Pleased to meet you, Judge." While having a black judge was not unusual when John had lived in New York City, it seemed like a rare thing for San Antonio.

"Mr. Crudder, I've already heard you brought in a prisoner that we're mighty glad to accommodate."

"Just call me John, Your Honor. I've just handed over Granger to the marshal."

"I can't tell you how glad we are to have him here. He's wanted for killin' one of our leading citizens, Mable Miller."

"I started trackin' him after he murdered an elderly couple in Bandera. Since then, I know he's killed more than twenty others and it may be many more than that. I have trouble keeping track of his crimes and I'm sure I don't know all of 'em."

John gave a quick recounting of the crimes Granger had committed. The judge listened solemnly. When John told about the way he had used dynamite on some of his victims, the judge let out a gasp.

The judge nodded as John finished describing Granger's exploits. "Since today is Friday, I'm gonna set the trial to begin on Monday mornin'. John, will you be able to stay over so you can give testimony of your capture of Granger?"

"I'd be glad to, Judge. Then as soon as the trial is over, I need to go to New Braunfels to pick up my horse before heading back to Bandera."

The marshal looked at the judge and smiled a bit. "Now there's one more matter that needs to be taken care of. There was a one-thousand-dollar reward for the capture of Granger. I think that money is yours and I think the judge will agree."

"I do indeed agree, Marshal. John, we don't have the money here but we can get it for you by Monday morning when the bank opens."

"Thanks just the same, gentlemen. But I've been very blessed in life and don't need the money. But I would like for the reward to be used on behalf of the families of the victims of Granger. Judge, do you think you might get someone in either the governor's office or the Texas Rangers to administer that?"

The judge nodded. "Yes, I can take care of that. With so many victims it will be split many ways but whatever they receive will be helpful."

John thanked the judge. "When I get back to Bandera, I'll supply some more money to help cover needs the needs of the families."

Crudder shook hands with both men and excused himself. He untied the chestnut horse from the hitching rail and rode to the telegraph office to let his family know he was safe and the journey was almost over. He also needed to tend to Midnight.

John arrived at the telegraph office and hurriedly wrote out the first telegram.

Slim Hanson
Bandera, Texas

Captured Granger. Trial starts Monday. Hope to be home in about a week. Love to Charlotte and the girls.

John Crudder
San Antonio, Texas

John wanted to send word that he would come for Midnight just as soon as he could but realized he didn't know the name of the livery stable or the stable hand's last name. Instead he wrote to the café across the street.

Naomi Kramer
Kramer's Kitchen
New Braunfels, Texas

Hope to return in a few days. Please ask Austin at the livery to take good care of my horse.

John Crudder
San Antonio

Crudder rode less than a mile to the Menger Hotel. He recalled how much he had enjoyed staying there in the past. When he checked in, he arranged to have a bath in the bathhouse behind the hotel. One thing he knew he would not be accepting was an offer for a cigar while he soaked as he did on his first stay at the Menger. His stomach ached as he remembered how sick he felt after that first cigar.

* * *

John spent Sunday walking around San Antonio. It felt odd not to have to worry about chasing Granger. He heard there was a new vaudeville theater in town. John recalled seeing vaudeville when he visited Paris during graduate school at Oxford.

He found the Jack Harris Saloon and Vaudeville Theater and purchased a ticket. John thoroughly enjoyed the performance and wished he could share it with Charlotte and the girls. Perhaps they would be able to go there on some future visit to San Antonio.

After the show, John rode back to the Menger, groomed his horse, and made arrangements for it to be stabled for the night. He requested that it be saddled by eight o'clock the next morning for the trial was scheduled to start at nine. That night, John rested well but realized how homesick he was. He couldn't wait to be back with his family on the H&F Ranch.

Roy Clinton

CHAPTER 23

The bailiff entered the court and said, "All rise. Hear ye, hear ye, hear ye. Let all who have business before the court draw near and ye shall be heard. The Honorable William A. Price presiding."

Judge Price walked into the courtroom, took his seat at the bench, and rapped his gavel once. "The only thing on the docket this morning is the matter of the State of Texas versus Butch Granger. Mr. Granger, what is your given name?"

Granger leaned forward and spit just as far as he could and shouted, "I ain't gonna be tried by no nig…."

Judge Price immediately rapped his gavel twice. "Granger, I'm finding you in contempt of court and fine you twenty-five dollars. Mr. Lopez, you will remind your client he shall accord himself to the decorum of the courtroom or I will have him bound and gagged throughout the rest of the trial. Is that clear?"

The attorney sitting beside Granger stood. "Yes, your honor. I'll make sure Mr. Granger understands." The attorney whispered loudly into Granger's ear.

The judge continued. "I see the defendant is here and represented by counsel. Also, the district attorney is here. Are both attorneys ready to proceed?"

The lawyers stood and responded at the same time. "Yes, your honor."

"Very well. Mr. Martinez, please call your first witness."

"Your honor, the state calls Chet Miller."

A man sitting in the first row behind the district attorney walked forward to the gate separating the bench from the rest of the courtroom. The bailiff approached him and held out a Bible. "Please place your hand on the Bible and swear to tell the truth."

"I'll tell the truth, your honor. I swear." He followed the instructions to have a seat in the witness stand and to state his full name.

The district attorney approached the witness stand. "Mr. Miller, I am sorry for the questions I must ask you for I know this is a painful time for you. But would you please repeat what you told me about the night your wife was murdered?"

Miller bowed his head and began to gather his thoughts. Tears dripped from his eyes and he started speaking. He took his arm and wiped way the tears. "My wife and I were at home when that man broke into our house." He pointed at Granger. "He asked us where our money was and my wife said we didn't have any money. Granger had a big smile on his face when he pulled out his gun and shot my wife twice. Once in the chest and once in the head." Miller wept as he recounted the horrific scene.

"What happened then, Mr. Miller?"

"Well, he—Granger—walked over to me and yelled, 'I want your money.' I was trying to check on my wife and Miller kicked me and yelled again for me to get the money. I went to the cookie jar and got the money Mable had been savin'. She had a little over thirty dollars."

The attorney waited patiently but when Miller didn't continue, he prompted him. "What happened next?"

"Mr. Freeman, who lives next door, came in with his shotgun. Granger had his gun on me and would have killed me if Mr. Freeman hadn't of chased him off."

"Thank you, Mr. Miller. I'll pass the witness, your honor."

"Mr. Lopez, you may cross examine."

"Thank you, your honor. Mr. Miller, isn't it true the man who shot your wife had a bandana covering his face?"

"Yes, sir."

"Isn't it also true that you were so distraught that you didn't get a good look at the killer?"

"No, sir. That's not true. I saw him just as plainly as I see him now. It was him. Granger. I would know him anywhere."

"But Mr. Miller, how could you so clearly identify him with the bandana covering his face?"

Miller looked at Granger and smiled. "Well, look at his ears. I've never met anyone whose ears look exactly like his. Also, when Mr. Freeman came in with his shotgun, Granger started to get away as quickly as he could. As he was goin' out, his bandana came down and I got a look at that evil smile he's always wearing. Just like he's smiling now."

The attorney realized he had already lost his case. "No more questions, your honor."

"Very well. Mr. Martinez, please call your next witness."

"Your honor, the state wishes to call Claude Freeman."

The bailiff came up and swore in Mr. Freeman who then took a seat in the witness stand. The district attorney approached him and began questioning him.

"Mr. Freeman, tell us what happened on the night Mrs. Miller was murdered."

Freeman was a tall man who filled out his frame. He was about thirty years old and had light, sandy-colored hair. "Well, I was just sitting at home with my wife when I heard a gunshot. I grabbed my shotgun and went outside. That's when I realized the sound was coming from the Miller's house next door. I ran to the house and burst through the door. I was afraid someone needed help so I went in without knocking."

"What happened next, Mr. Freeman?"

"I saw Mrs. Miller on the floor covered in blood. And I saw that man with his gun out like he was gettin' ready to shoot Mr. Miller. So, I pulled back the hammers on my shotgun and took aim at Granger. He high-tailed it out of there. And it's a good thing he did 'cause I would have killed him shor 'nough."

"And did you get a clear look at the defendant's face?"

"Yes, I did. When he started to run, his bandana slipped down and I saw his face. He was sneerin' at me the way he is now."

"No more questions, your honor."

"Mr. Lopez, you may question the witness."

Lopez stood and walked toward the witness stand. "Mr. Freeman, thank you for coming today. I know you have gone through a harrowing time. Now in the confusion, isn't it just possible that you didn't see the face of the murderer at all? Isn't it possible you were just influenced by seeing the defendant here and you thought you had seen his face at the Miller's house?"

"No. I know what I saw. You can't make it out to be no other way. I saw him." Freeman raised his voice as he pointed at Granger. "He was there and was holdin' his gun on Mr. Miller, just like I said."

Santiago Lopez looked dejectedly at the judge. "No other questions, your honor."

"Call your next witness, Mr. Martinez."

"The state calls Miss Louise Granger." A very surprised young woman walked to the front of the courtroom. The bailiff swore her in and escorted her to the witness stand.

Pablo Martinez smiled as he walked to the witness stand to address the young woman. "Miss Granger, do you live here in San Antonio?"

"Yes, I do but I don't know anything about what's going on at this trial. I don't have anything I can add, your honor." She looked pleadingly to the judge. "I think there's some mistake. There's no reason for me to be called as a witness."

"I object," said Lopez. "Miss Granger has nothing to do with this case."

"Your honor," said Martinez. "I'll show the relevancy of this line of questioning in a few minutes if you'll grant me just a few questions."

"Very well," said the judge. "But I don't abide wild goose chases, Mr. Martinez. Make sure you can tie this together. And do it soon."

"Yes, sir, your honor. So, Miss Granger, can you please tell us where you live?"

"I live over on Third Street."

"And Miss Granger, can you tell me your relationship to the defendant?"

"I'm his baby—I mean younger sister. He's fifteen years older than me."

"Would you tell us when you communicated with him last?"

"I haven't seen him in, I don't know, maybe five years."

"Have you had any communication with him since that time?"

"Yes, I sometimes write him letters. He doesn't write back but I want him to know I haven't forgotten about him."

"And can you please tell the jury when you wrote him last?"

Louise thought for a moment. "I think it was about a month ago."

Martinez walked back to his desk and picked up a letter that he handed to Miss Granger. "And is this the letter?"

Louise examined the envelope and then pulled the letter out. "Yes, that's the last one I wrote him." She handed it back to Martinez who handed it to the judge for his inspection.

"Thank you, Miss Granger. No further questions, your honor."

The judge looked at Granger's attorney. "Mr. Lopez, you may cross examine the witness."

Lopez quickly stood. "No questions, your honor."

"Mr. Martinez, you may call your next witness."

"The state wishes to call Mr. John Crudder to the stand."

When the bailiff had sworn him in, John took a seat in the witness stand.

The district attorney walked up to John. "Mr. Crudder, I understand you captured Granger making a citizen's arrest, and brought him to San Antonio. Please tell the jury why you took it upon yourself to track down Butch Granger."

Crudder cleared his throat and started his story. "I went by the marshal's office in Bandera a few weeks ago. Mayor Hanson was there with the marshal. Anyway, they told me they had just come from the Jackson farm out east of town. They said the Jackson's were murdered and robbed. Mrs. Jackson was shot and then her body blown up by dynamite. The mayor said he thought Butch Granger was the murderer."

Lopez jumped to his feet. "I object your honor. First, this witness is giving hearsay testimony and there is no foundation for the accusation he is making."

Martinez addressed the judge. "Your honor, I can make the connection if you will allow me a bit of latitude."

"Very well, Mr. Martinez. But don't go chasin' rabbits. Make your point and be quick about it."

"Yes, your honor." Martinez turned toward Crudder. "Why did the mayor think the murderer was Butch Granger?"

"Because they found the letter from Louise Granger addressed to Butch Granger by the body of Jack Jackson. That's the letter that I gave to you."

"And it's the same letter Miss Granger said she wrote?"

Crudder nodded, "That's right."

Martinez continued, "Was there anything else you would like to say?"

Crudder looked at Granger. "The mayor of Bandera went to school with Granger. He said Granger used to delight in killing pets and other animals. The kids called him The Butcher and then shortened it to Butch and the name stuck."

Lopez jumped to his feet. "I strenuously object, your honor. This testimony is second hand and has no relevance to the trial."

The judge nodded. "That may well be but I'm gonna allow it. We can always get the mayor of Bandera to come here and testify if we need to. Please proceed, Mr. Martinez."

Martinez again addressed Crudder. "Were there other crimes you discovered as you chased Mr. Granger?"

For the next twenty minutes, John recounted the many heartless murders Granger had committed. He described the killings in detail, often causing the jury to look away in horror. John reported the descriptions given by survivors and how they all pointed to Granger. Several times Santiago Lopez objected but was not successful in getting the judge to exclude any of John's testimony.

When John left the witness stand, the prosecution rested its case. Lopez did his best to bring a defense but everyone in the courtroom, including the defendant, knew the effort was wasted. The jury was sent to deliberate and only took ten minutes to return a verdict of guilty. After reading the verdict, the judge rapped his gavel several times to quiet down the courtroom that had erupted with shouts and cheers.

"Before I pass sentence on Granger, I want to address Mr. Miller." The judge turned so he was directly addressing the husband of the murder victim. "Mr. Miller, I think I know the sentence you hope will be passed here today. I'm sorry it will not be as you hoped. But I hope you will be able to follow my reasoning and find comfort in knowing that justice will be served."

Judge Price turned toward Granger. "Will the defendant please rise?" Both Granger and Lopez stood. "Butch 'The Butcher' Granger. I received a telegram from the Texas Rangers of the many towns and cities where you are wanted for murder, bank robbery, and the wholesale, wanton, slaughter of cattle and horses. You're a man who is both amoral and lacking a conscience. And for that, you deserve to hang by the neck until dead.

"However, that is not the sentence I give you today, though that is what I would like to pass. To give you that sentence and rapidly carry that out would deprive the families of many other victims from getting a chance to speak against you in a court of law. Therefore, today, I sentence you to life in the Texas State Penitentiary in Huntsville, without the possibility of parole."

There was an immediate outcry in the courtroom as people reacted to the sentence. Judge Price banged his gavel on the bench. "Court is dismissed."

Granger stood and lunged at the judge as his attorney tried to restrain him. "I'm gonna kill you, Judge." Granger yelled insults and profanities at the judge as the bailiff subdued him and handcuffed his hands behind his back. Turning toward his attorney he continued his verbal attack. "And Lopez, I'm gonna kill you too and then I'm gonna kill your family.

Butch Granger was raised to his feet to be ushered off to jail. His eyes found Crudder and his sneer intensified. "And you, John Crudder. I'm gonna escape from prison and I'm comin' for you. I'll kill you and your family and will enjoy every moment." The bailiff and the marshal each grabbed Granger's arms and pulled him down the aisle. "Mark my word, Crudder. I'm gonna make you pay for bringin' me in. And before I finish with you, you're gonna wish you never heard of The Butcher. I'm gonna butcher you all."

The remaining spectators couldn't believe what they were hearing. Several women had their hands to their mouths. Most of the men were getting as far as possible from the horrible man as though they were afraid he would break out of his restraints and attack them.

When Granger was finally out of the courtroom, the judge sat in silence and contemplated Granger's outburst. Santiago Lopez was visibly shaken. John Crudder made a mental note of the threat. He felt sure if Granger ever did escape, he would try to carry out his threats. But for now, Crudder was glad his work was done.

John shook hands with Marshal Dobbin and swung up onto his chestnut horse and headed back to New Braunfels. He was looking forward to finding out how Midnight was recovering from pneumonia. It was more than thirty miles and John knew it would take him the rest of the day to get there.

* * *

Immediately upon arriving in New Braunfels, John went to the livery stable. He had no sooner tied the chestnut to the hitching rail than Austin appeared.

"Howdy, John. Did you come to visit me or is there some other reason for your visit?" The stable hand laughed at his own humor.

"Howdy, Austin. How's the patient?"

"You're not gonna believe it but your horse is as good as new. The doc's back with him now."

John hurriedly made his way around the other horses in the stable to make it to Midnight's stall. John let out a little whistle on the way and Midnight immediately nickered in response. Doc Shriver turned to greet John. "Hello, Mr. Crudder. Come to see a happy and healthy horse?"

"Howdy, Doc. How's he doin'?"

"Couldn't be any better. He ran a fever for only one day and now he's fully recovered. I've never known a horse to throw off pneumonia as quickly as Midnight."

John stroked his beautiful mount and wrapped both arms around his neck. "When do you think I can ride him again?"

"You can ride him now. In fact, he can run now. Like I said, he's fully recovered."

John and Doc Shriver continued talking about Midnight's health. John paid the doctor for his services and then made a deal to sell the chestnut back to Austin. John told him he would be leaving first thing in the morning so he went ahead and settled his livery bill.

John walked across the street to Kramer's and took a seat in the dining room. The waitress came to his table and greeted him. "Hello, Mr. Crudder. I'm so glad you've come back."

"Hello, Miss Charlotte. What's good to eat this evenin'?"

"Tonight, we have chicken and dumplings. I think you'll like them."

"That sounds fine. I think I'll have some. Would you mind if I stick my head in the kitchen to speak to your mother?"

"Go right ahead. That will be fine."

John walked to the kitchen door, knocked softly and then pushed the door open. "Hello, Mrs. Kramer."

"Good evening, Mr. Crudder. I'm glad you made it safely back to our little town. How may I help you?"

"I just wanted to thank you for delivering the message to Austin about my horse. I didn't know Austin's last name and I didn't know the name of the livery stable. The only way I could think of to get word to Austin was through you."

Naomi smiled at John. "I was glad to do it. I know a cowboy's horse is special to him and I know yours had been ill. It was a pleasure to help you, sir."

John returned to his seat just as Charlotte brought his chicken and dumplings. "I just made a pitcher of lemonade. Would you like a glass?"

"Yes, that would be fine. Thank you." John finished his bowl and accepted an offer for seconds. He left a generous tip on the table for Charlotte and walked to the hotel next door.

"Mr. Kramer, I'd like to settle my bill. I owe you for the room I rented for a week and I do need a room for one more night. And, of course, I owe for the meals I've eaten. And be sure to add two servings of chicken 'n dumplin's and a lemonade for tonight."

Kramer greeted John in return and did a quick calculation. John paid his bill and added some additional money to thank his wife for the great meals and for delivering the message to the stable man.

As John turned in for the night, he thought about home and about his wife and children. He knew Midnight could make the trip to Bandera in a day but he was going to take it easy and spend one night on the trail. Turning out his lamp, John lay on his bed and smiled at the thought of seeing his family in only a couple of days. But as he slept that night, he dreamed of Granger breaking out of prison

Roy Clinton

EPILOGUE

Bandera, Texas

John arrived home near dusk after spending two days in the saddle. Midnight did seem back to his old self. He wanted to run, but John held him to a trot and walk most of the way while occasionally letting him lope. As he pulled up to the hitching rail, both daughters ran to the porch. "Daddy," they cried out together.

He swung down from Midnight and grabbed a daughter in each arm. "And how are my favorite daughters doin'?"

"I love you, Daddy," said Claire.

"Me too," said Cora.

Charlotte came out to the porch followed by Richie and Slim. John placed his daughters on the porch and enveloped Charlotte in his arms.

"John, I'm so glad you're home." Charlotte hugged him back with all her might.

Over Charlotte's shoulder, John spoke to the rest of his family.

"Howdy, Richie. Hello, Slim."

"We're all happy you're home," said Richie.

Slim walked over and patted John on the back. "And I'm especially glad you captured Granger. Hopefully that's the last we'll hear of him."

Charlotte pulled back out of the embrace and looked at the bruises on John's face. Though she didn't say so, she wondered what other wounds his clothes were covering. "Come on in, John. We were just sitting down to eat. I think you're gonna enjoy it. We're having chicken and dumplings. And I just made a pitcher of lemonade." John followed her into the house with a big smile on his face. "Why are you smiling? What's so amusing?"

That night, John went to bed knowing he had everything he wanted in life. Just before he fell asleep, Charlotte nudged him. "Tomorrow's a big day."

"Why's that?" asked John.

"You know whose birthday it is?"

John thought, worried that he might have missed his wife's birthday. Charlotte laughed as she saw the consternation on his face. "It's Daddy's birthday. And you know who else is having a birthday? Richie."

"You mean they both have birthdays on the same day?" Isn't that something.

Charlotte continued. "And you know how we're going to celebrate? We're having a fiesta and Daddy and Slim are doing all the cooking. We're inviting several friends out and some of the hands are going to join us. It will be a great party."

* * *

Charlotte heard someone riding up so she got up to great the new guest. Marshal Williams trotted his horse to the hitching rail, swung down, and walked up to the porch. "Evenin', Charlotte. Is there any food left?"

"Of course, there is, Marshal. Come on in. We have just started."

He walked into the living room. "Howdy, everybody. I shor hope there's some food left 'cause I'm powerful hungry."

"Howdy, Marshal," said Slim. "Fill your plate and then come join us at our table." Clem wasted no time filling his plate and taking the empty seat. After several bites, he spoke up.

"I almost forgot. I've got two telegrams for John. Let me find it. Here they are." Instead of handing the telegrams to Crudder, he cleared his voice and read it out loud.

John Crudder
Bandera, Texas

Fredericksburg courthouse money to be delivered by stage. Alvelda is healing nicely. Sends her love.

Howard Hastings
Fifth Avenue, New York City

John smiled as he thought about the surprise that would

soon arrive for his friend in Fredericksburg. When he heard of Alvelda's continued recovery, he let out a sigh of relief. Then Marshall Williams read the second telegram.

John Crudder
Bandera, Texas

Come immediately. Bring MM.

Jeffrey Jameson
Washington, D.C.

Clem continued eating as he finished reading the second telegram. In between mouthfuls, the marshal looked over at Crudder. "John, who do you know in Washington, D.C.? And who is MM?"

Charlotte and John exchanged a look as Slim tried to change the subject. "Charlotte, why don't you refill the Marshal's plate. Do you think you have room for seconds, Clem?"

The End

ACKNOWLEDGMENTS

I would like to say thanks to my wife, Kathie, who was the first to read this book and give helpful edits and encouragement throughout the writing process. We thoroughly enjoy our research trips through Texas to make sure the books portray the cities and various parts of the state accurately.

I would also like to thank the Top Westerns Publishing team: Teresa Lauer, publisher who also designs the books and works through hundreds of details to make sure we meet deadlines; Sharon Smith, copy editor, whose work makes me appear more literate; Maxwell Morelli, substantive editor, whose job it is to make sure the parts fit together properly and to ensure continuity of the series; Laurie Barboza, for her creative cover designs; and R. William James, who produces the audio versions of each book. I would also like to thank the great beta readers, Faye Lewis, Chris Bryan, Michael Porter, Phil Lauer, and Teresa Lauer. Your suggestions helped make this novel better.

If you have an eye for detail and think you would like to be a beta reader, get manuscripts before anyone else, and have a chance to shape the final book, please email me at Roy@TopWesterns.com and I'll let you know what is involved.

As with my other books, I have sought to be historically

accurate in as many details as possible. The city of Bee Cave (originally called Bee Caves when the post office opened there in 1870) is beautifully situated on the confluence of Barton Creek and Little Barton Creek.

After being known as Du Pre, Texas, for six years, the United States post office discovered there was another town named Du Pre and required the town to change its name. The name was changed to Buda, Texas. Supposedly, the name is a mispronunciation of the Spanish word "viuda" or "widow."

Camp Verde was a US Army post and the home to many camels. Stories of the experiment with the animals abound there today. Some residents even claim there are some decedents of the original camels roaming the countryside.

In New Braunfels, Texas, you can visit Saints Peter and Paul Church. It was indeed built just a couple of years before John Crudder rode into the town. In San Antonio, the marshal at that time really was John Dobbin; and Judge William A. Price, who served at that time, really was the first African American judge in the city.

I'm always glad to hear from readers. You may email me at Roy@TopWesterns.com. I make it a point to answer every letter. Please be patient if it takes me a few days to respond. I may be on a writing retreat or traveling, but I will reply.

The next book in the *Midnight Marauder* series will be released soon. The title is *Candy Man*. This is a historical novel of the first kidnapping for ransom in the United States. I think you will like the role the Midnight Marauder plays in this book. You may read a preview on the next few pages. Also, you can listen to audio versions of all the Top Western books on Audible.com and on iTunes. Audible versions are available one to two months after the release of the digital and printed versions.

Roy Clinton

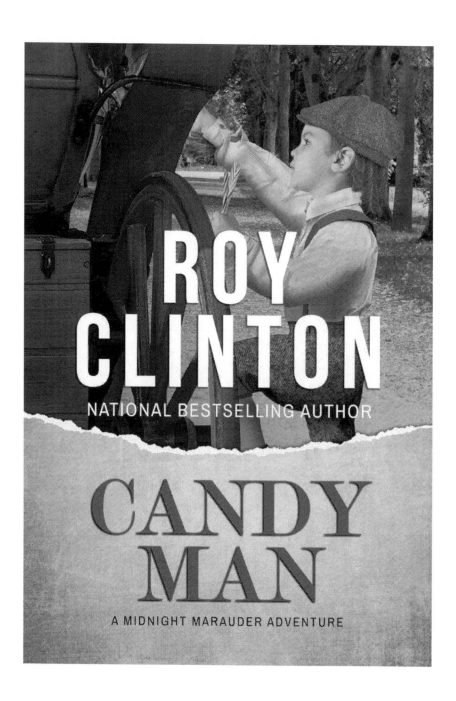

ROY
CLINTON

NATIONAL BESTSELLING AUTHOR

CANDY
MAN

A MIDNIGHT MARAUDER ADVENTURE

Roy Clinton

CANDY MAN

A Midnight Marauder Adventure

Roy Clinton

1874

PROLOGUE

Wednesday, June 24th
Brooklyn Heights, New York

The saloon was dark and stank of stale beer. Bill sat on a stool, as per his instructions, and waited. It was the middle of the morning. The only people in a saloon this time of morning either had no other place they needed to be or they were booze hounds who couldn't hold a job.

"What are you having?" The bartender seemed bored with his job and not the least bit interested in what Bill wanted. To him, Bill was just another interruption in his day. Another customer who would make demands on his time, drink a few beers, make a mess, and then leave without so much as a 'thank you' or a tip.

"Beer." As Bill ordered his drink, he slowly looked around the saloon, wondering who he was meeting. There were a few patrons but no one who was paying any attention to him. At the far end of the bar, Bill spotted someone he thought might be his contact. He waited but the man never looked his way.

He thought back to the letter he received and wondered how anyone had selected him. Reaching in his pocket, he retrieved the letter that he found on the deck of his boat. Someone had left it near the gangplank and weighted with a rock.

Want to make some big money? Meet me on Wednesday, June 24th at 10:00 a.m. in the saloon at 62 Montague Street between, Pierrepont Place and Hicks Street. Tell no one. Sit at bar and wait. I'll contact you.

Bill fingered the letter and wondered who sent it. When it talked about big money, he wondered how much that really meant. He refolded the letter and placed it back in his pocket and took a sip of his beer. Bill had never really acquired a taste for beer but he wanted to fit in. Ordering anything else would have made him standout.

Fifteen minutes passed and still no one had showed the slightest interest in him. No new customers had entered since he arrived. Bill wondered if he had the wrong day. Once again, he removed the letter from his pocket and verified the date for the meeting.

From the back corner of the saloon, a man approached the

bartender and ordered another beer. As he was taking it back toward his table, he made eye contact with Bill and gave the smallest indication with his head he should follow. Bill picked up his beer and followed the stranger.

The stranger took a long swallow of his beer and set it back on the table. Bill noticed the man was wearing expensive clothes. He wore a beautifully tailored suit and had a beaver top hat and an ivory inlaid cane on the table. The stranger's shirt looked to be made of silk as did his black tie.

He looked at Bill as though he were trying to see into his soul. Bill was self-conscious about his appearance. He knew he was not a handsome man and his clothes were well-worn and dirty.

As Bill watched, the stranger withdrew his wallet from the inside pocket of his suit coat. He withdrew ten, hundred-dollar bills and slid them across the table. Bill's eyes grew large and he could feel his heart race as he eyed the money. While he had seen hundred-dollar bills before, he had never seen ten of them, much less thought he would ever be able to call them his own.

"What's that far? What do I have to do?"

The stranger furtively looked from side to side. Confident they were not being overheard, the stranger laid out his plan.

"That's expense money. There is a child you're going to snatch. The family will give you twenty thousand dollars to get him back. Half the money will be mine and the other half will be yours. Do you have any problem with taking a child?"

Bill didn't hesitate. "None whatsoever. But I don't see why I will need to spend any of this money on expenses. I can just snatch the child and wait for his parents to pay."

"This is not going to be so simple of a job. First of all, the child is in Philadelphia. And secondly, you're going to need help. I want you to find some men to help you. However, you can never mention me. They are not to even know I exist. So far as they are concerned, the kidnapping is all your idea.

"You're not to get in a hurry. Careful planning will make this the perfect crime. No one has ever done this before. You'll be the first. Do you think you can do that?"

Bill's mouth slowly turned to a smile. "Of course, I can. And I'm a real good planner. Where do I find this child?"

"You and your accomplices are to go to this address in Philadelphia." The stranger slid a piece of paper across to Bill. "The boy's name is Charles Brewster Ross and he is four years old. They call him Charlie. His father is Christian Ross. On Friday, June twenty-sixth, Mr. Ross is sending his wife and three of his children on summer vacation to Atlantic City. That will just leave Charlie, Walter, and the baby at home with their father. As soon after that as possible, I want you to take Charlie and then get someone to take care of him in a secret location."

Bill listened and took in all he was being told. "Here is a map to a cave about thirty miles north of Philadelphia. I already have it stocked with food, blankets, and other supplies. There is a little stream right beside it so you will have plenty of water. It is in the middle of nowhere. Your man can keep Charlie safe there for as long as it necessary."

"How will we ever be able to keep him quiet while taking

him to the cave? He's likely to be screaming his lungs out."

The stranger pulled a brown bottle from his coat and set it on the table. "This is chloroform. You put a little bit on a cloth and have him breathe it and he will be out in an instant. Just don't use too much and don't use it more than necessary."

Mosher pulled the stopped from the bottle and sniffed it. "It smells sweet."

"Don't do that, fool. One more breath and you won't smell anything because you will be out cold." Mosher put the cork back in the bottle and refolded the map and then put both items in his pocket.

The stranger looked intently at Mosher. "This is important. The boy is not to be harmed in any way. If he is harmed, you will answer to me. And you don't want to see what I do when I get angry."

Bill nodded his head in agreement. His eyes moved back and forth as he formulated a plan. "I think I want two, maybe three more men to help me. I can see how they can help me get the lay of the land. And it will probably take two men to get him to the cave and take care of him."

"Now you see why you need expense money. You'll need to get to Philadelphia and you'll need to have money for food and lodging while you plan your job and then while we're waiting for Mr. Ross to pay."

Bill looked intently at the stranger. "I don't even know your name."

"No, you don't. And you're not going to. All you need from

me is the address of the child and money for expenses. After you take the child, you're to write a letter to Mr. Ross—disguise it as best you can—and demand twenty thousand dollars for the return of Charlie."

"How am I supposed to contact you?"

"You'll not need to contact me. I'll know what you're doing. I'll know when you take the boy and when you've been paid for his return. When you get the money, I'll let you know where we're to meet."

Bill took a swallow of his beer and made a face as he tasted its bitterness. "When do I get started?"

The stranger stood, picked up his cane, placed his hat on his head and said, "Now." Bill watched as the stranger walked out of the saloon, then he smiled as he picked up the stack of bills on the table. For the first time in his life, he felt rich.

Here's how :
1) go to amazon.com
2) search for Roy Clinton
3) click on appropriate title
4) write a review

The review you write will help get the word out to others who may benefit.

– Thanks for your help,
Roy Clinton